Patrolman Genero was brushing water from his trousers when he saw the bag resting on the sidewalk alongside the bus stop sign. He walked to the sign and picked up the bag. It was not very heavy. An identification tag showed behind a celluloid panel, but whoever owned the bag had neglected to fill in the name and address spaces. Sourly, Genero unzipped the bag and reached in it. *He drew back his hand in terror and revulsion. And then he gripped the bus stop sign for support because he was suddenly dizzy. . . .*

The old woman lifted the lid of the garbage can and prepared to toss her bag into it and run like hell for the shelter of her building. Then she saw the newspaper. She hesitated for a moment. The newspaper had been wrapped around something, but the wrapping had come loose. Curiously the old lady bent closer to the garbage can. *And then she let out a shriek. . . .*

Give the Boys
a Great Big Hand

An 87th Precinct Mystery

by Ed McBain

A SIGNET BOOK

NEW AMERICAN LIBRARY

A DIVISION OF PENGUIN BOOKS USA INC.

This is for Phyllis and Rick

Published by arrangement with Ed McBain

SIGNET TRADEMARK REG. U.S. PAT. OFF. AND FOREIGN COUNTRIES
REGISTERED TRADEMARK—MARCA REGISTRADA
HECHO EN DRESDEN, TN

SIGNET, SIGNET CLASSIC, MENTOR, ONYX, PLUME, MERIDIAN and NAL BOOKS are published by New American Library, a division of Penguin Books USA Inc., 1633 Broadway, New York, New York 10019

FIRST PRINTING, SEPTEMBER, 1975

6 7 8 9 10 11 12 13 14

PRINTED IN THE UNITED STATES OF AMERICA

One

IT WAS RAINING.

It had been raining for three days now, an ugly March rain that washed the brilliance of near-spring with a monochromatic, unrelenting gray. The television forecasters had correctly predicted rain for today and estimated that it would rain tomorrow also. Beyond that, they would not venture an opinion.

But it seemed to Patrolman Richard Genero that it had been raining forever, and that it would continue to rain forever, and that eventually he would be washed away into the gutters and then carried into the sewers of Isola and dumped unceremoniously with the other garbage into either the River Harb or the River Dix. North or south, it didn't make a damn bit of difference: both rivers were polluted; both stank of human waste.

Like a man up to his ankles in water in a rapidly sinking rowboat, Genero stood on the corner and surveyed the near-empty streets. His rubber rain cape was as black and as shining as the asphalt that stretched before him. It was still early afternoon, but there was hardly a soul in sight, and Genero felt lonely and deserted. He felt, too, as if he were the only human being in the entire city who didn't know enough to come in out of the rain. I'm going to drown here in the goddamn streets, he thought, and he belched sourly, consoling himself with the fact that he would be relieved on post at 3:45. It would take him about five minutes to get back to the station house and no more than ten minutes to change into his street clothes. Figure a half hour on the subway to Riverhead, and he would be home at 4:30. He wouldn't have to pick up Gilda until 7:30, so that gave him time for a little nap before dinner. Thinking of the nap, Genero yawned, tilting his head.

A drop of cold water ran down his neck, and he said, "Oh hell!" out loud, and then hurriedly glanced around him to make sure he hadn't been overheard by any conscientious citizen of the city. Satisfied that the image of the pure American law-enforcer had not been destroyed, Genero began walking up the street, his rubber-encased shoes sloshing water every inch of the way.

Rain, rain, go away, he thought.

Oddly, the rain persisted.

Well, rain isn't so bad, he thought. It's better than snow, anyway. The thought made him shudder a little, partially because the very thought of snow was a chilling one, and partially because he could never think of snow or winter without forming an immediate association with the boy he had found in the basement so long ago.

Now cut that out, he thought. It's bad enough it's raining. We don't have to start thinking of creepy cadavers.

The boy's face had been blue, really blue, and he'd been leaning forward on the cot, and it had taken Genero several moments to realize that a rope was around the boy's neck and that the boy was dead.

Listen, let's not even think about it. It makes me itchy.

Well, listen, you're a cop, he reminded himself. What do you think cops do? Turn off fire hydrants all the time? Break up stickball games? I mean, now let's face it, every now and then a cop has got to find a stiff.

Listen, this makes me itchy.

I mean, that's what you get paid for, man. I mean, let's face it. A cop has every now and then got to come up against a little violence. And besides, that kid was a long time ago, all water under the . . .

Water. Jesus, ain't it never going to stop raining?

I'm getting out of this rain, he thought. I'm going over to Max's tailor shop and maybe I can get him to take out some of that sweet Passover wine, and we'll drink a toast to Bermuda. Man, I wish I was in Bermuda. He walked down the street and opened the door to the tailor shop. A bell tinkled. The shop smelled of steam and clean garments.

Genero felt better the moment he stepped inside.

"Hello, Max," he said.

Max was a round-faced man with a fringe of white hair that clung to his balding pate like a halo. He looked up from his sewing machine and said, "I ain't got no wine."

"Who wants wine?" Genero answered, grinning a bit sheepishly. "Would you kick me out of your shop on a miserable day like this?"

"On any day, miserable or otherwise, I wouldn't kick you out mine shop," Max said, "so don't make wisecracks. But I warn you, already, even before you begin, I ain't got no wine."

"So who wants wine?" Genero said. He moved closer to the radiator and pulled off his gloves. "What are you doing, Max?"

"What does it look like I'm doing? I'm making a plan for the White House. I'm going to blow it up. What else would I be doing on a sewing machine?"

"I mean, what's that thing you're working on?"

"It's a Salvation Army uniform," Max said.

"Yeah? How about that?"

"There's still a few *tailors* left in this city, you know," Max said. "It ain't by all of us a matter of cleaning and pressing. Cleaning and pressing is for machines. Tailoring is for men. Max Mandel is a tailor, not a pressing machine."

"And a damn good tailor," Genero said, and he watched for Max's reaction.

"I still ain't got no wine," Max said. "Why ain't you in the street stopping crime already?"

"On a day like this, nobody's interested in crime," Genero said. "The only crime going on today is prostitution."

Genero watched Max's face, saw the quick gleam of appreciation in the old man's eyes and grinned. He was getting closer to that wine all the time. Max was beginning to enjoy his jokes, and that was a good sign. Now all he had to do was work up a little sympathy.

"A rain like today's," Genero said, "it seeps right into a man's bones. Right into his bones."

"So?"

"So nothing. I'm just saying. Right to the marrow. And the worst part is, a man can't even stop off in a bar or something to get a shot. To warm him up, I mean. It ain't allowed, you know."

"So?"

"So nothing. I'm just saying." Genero paused. "You're sure doing a fine job with that uniform, Max."

"Thanks."

The shop went silent. Outside, the rain spattered against the sidewalk in continuous drumming monotony.

"Right to the marrow," Genero said.

"All right already. Right to the marrow."

"Chills a man."

"All right, it chills a man."

"Yes, sir," Genero said, shaking his head.

"The wine is in the back near the pressing machine," Max said without looking up. "Don't drink too much, you'll get drunk already and I'll be arrested for corrupting an officer."

"You mean you have wine, Max?" Genero asked innocently.

"Listen to Mr. Baby-Blue Eyes, he's asking if I got wine. Go, go in the back. Drink, choke, but leave some in the bottle."

"That's awfully nice of you, Max," Genero said, beaming. "I had no idea you—"

"Go, go before I change my mind."

Genero went into the back room and found the bottle of wine on the table near the pressing machine. He uncapped it, rinsed a glass at the sink near the small grime-smeared window and poured it full to the brim. He tilted the glass to his mouth, drank until it was empty, and then licked his lips.

"You want some of this, Max?" he called.

"The Salvation Army doesn't like I should drink when I'm sewing their uniforms."

"It's very good, Max," Genero said teasingly.

"So have another glass and stop bothering me. You're making my stiches go all *fermisht*."

Genero drank another glassful, recapped the bottle, and

came out into the shop again, rubbing his hands briskly.

"Now I'm ready for anything," he said, grinning.

"What is there to be ready for? On a day like this, you already said there's nothing but prostitution."

"I'm ready for that, too," Genero answered. "Come on, Max. Close up the shop, and we'll go find two delicious broads. What do you say?"

"Stop giving an old man ideas. My wife should only find me with a delicious broad. A knife she'll stick in my back. Get out, get out, go walk your beat. Go arrest the other drunkards and vagrants. Leave me in peace. I'm running here a bar and grill instead of a tailor shop. Every drunkard cop on the beat, he stops in for wine. The government should allow me to deduct the wine as part of my overhead. One day, in the wine bottle, I'm going to put poison instead of wine. Then maybe the *fercockteh* cops of the 87th will leave me alone, already. Go. Get lost. Go."

"Ahhh, you know you love us, Max."

"I love you like cockroaches."

"Better than cockroaches."

"That's right. I love you like water rats."

Genero pulled on his gloves. "Well, back to the bridge," he said.

"What bridge?"

"The bridge of the ship. That's a joke, Max. The rain, get it? Water. A ship. Get it?"

"Already the television world lost a great comic when you decided to be a cop," Max said, shaking his head. "Back to the bridge." He shook his head again. "Do me a favor, will you?"

"What's that?" Genero asked, opening the door.

"From the bridge of this ship . . ."

"Yeah?"

"Jump!"

Genero grinned and closed the door behind him. It was still pouring outside, but he felt a lot better now. The sweet wine fumed in his stomach, and he could feel a warm lassitude seeping through his limbs. He sloshed through the puddles in an almost carefree manner, squinting through the driving rain, whistling tunelessly.

The man—or perhaps the tall woman, it was difficult to tell—was standing at the bus stop. The tall woman—or perhaps the man, it was impossible to see clearly in the rain —was dressed entirely in black. Black raincoat, black slacks, black shoes, black umbrella which effectively hid the head and hair. The bus pulled to the curb, spreading a huge canopy of water. The doors snapped open. The person—man or woman—boarded the bus and the rain-streaked doors closed again, hiding the black-shrouded fig-ure from view. The bus pulled away from the curb, spread-ing another canopy of water which soaked Genero's trouser legs.

"You stupid . . ." he shouted, and he began brushing water from his trousers, and that was when he saw the bag resting on the sidewalk alongside the bus stop sign.

"Hey! Hey!" he yelled after the bus. "You forgot your bag!"

His words were drowned in the gunning roar of the bus's engine and the steady drumming of the rain.

"Damnit," he muttered, and he walked to the sign and picked up the bag. It was a small, blue overnight bag, ob-viously issued by an airline. In a white circle on the side of the bag, stenciled there in red letters, were the words: CIR-CLE AIRLINES.

Beneath that, in white script lettering, was the slogan: *We circle the globe.*

Genero studied the bag. It was not very heavy. A small leather fob was attached to the carrying straps, and an identification tag showed behind a celluloid panel. But whoever owned the bag had neglected to fill in the NAME and ADDRESS spaces. The identification tag was blank.

Sourly, Genero unzipped the bag and reached into it.

He drew back his hand in terror and revulsion. An in-stant thought rushed across his mind—God, not again—and then he gripped the bus stop sign for support because he was suddenly dizzy.

Two

In the detective squadroom of the 87th Precinct, the boys were swapping reminiscences about their patrolman days.

Now you may quarrel with the use of the word "boys" to describe a group of men who ranged in age from twenty-eight to forty-two, who shaved daily, who went to bed with various and assorted mature and immature women, who swore like pirates, and who dealt with some of the dirtiest humans since Neanderthal. The word "boys," perhaps, connotes a simplicity, an innocence which would not be entirely accurate.

There was, however, a spirit of boyish innocence in the squadroom on that dreary, rainy March day. It was difficult to believe that these men who stood in a fraternal knot around Andy Parker's desk, grinning, listening in attentiveness, were men who dealt daily with crime and criminals. The squadroom, in effect, could have been a high-school locker room. The chatter could have been that of a high-school football team on the day of the season's last game. The men stood drinking coffee from carboard containers, completely at ease in the grubby shopworn comfort of the squadroom. Andy Parker, like a belligerent fullback remembering a difficult time in the game against Central High, kept his team huddled about him, leaned back in his swivel chair, and shook his head dolefully.

"I had a pipperoo one time, believe me," he said. "I stopped her coming off the River Highway. Right near Pier 17, do you know the spot?"

The boys nodded.

"Well, she crashed the light at the bottom of the ramp,

11

and then made a U-turn under the highway. I blew the whistle, and she jammed on the brakes, and I strolled over to the car and said, 'Lady, you must be the Mayor's daughter to be driving like that.' "

"Was she?" Steve Carella asked. Sitting on the edge of the desk, a lean muscular man with eyes that slanted peculiarly downward to present an Oriental appearance, he held his coffee container in big hands and studied Parker intently. He did not particularly care for the man or his methods of police investigation, but he had to admit he told a story with gusto.

"No, no. Mayor's daughter, my eye. What she was— well, let me tell the story, will you?"

Parker scratched his heavy beard. He had shaved that morning, but five o'clock shadow came at an earlier hour for him, so that he always looked somewhat unkempt, a big shaggy man with dark hair, dark eyes, dark beard. In fact, were it not for the shield Parker carried pinned to his wallet, he could easily have passed for many of the thieves who found their way into the 87th. He was so much the Hollywood stereotype of the gangster that he'd often been stopped by overzealous patrolmen seeking suspicious characters. On those occasions, he immediately identified himself as a detective and then proceeded to bawl out the ambitious rookie, which pastime—though he never admitted it to himself—gave him a great deal of pleasure. In truth, it was possible that Andy Parker purposely roamed around in other precincts hoping to be stopped by an unsuspecting patrolman upon whom he could then pull his rank.

"She was sitting in the front seat with a two-piece costume on," Parker said, "a two-piece costume and these long black net stockings. What the costume was, it was these little black panties covered with sequins, and this tiny little bra that tried to cover the biggest set of bubs I ever seen on any woman in my entire life I swear to God. I did a double take, and I leaned into the car and said, 'You just passed a stop light, lady, and you made a U-turn over a double white line. And for all I know, we got a good case against you for indecent exposure. Now how about that?' "

"What did she say?" Cotton Hawes asked. He alone of

the detectives surrounding Parker's desk was not drinking coffee. Hawes was a tea drinker, a habit he'd picked up as a growing boy. His father had been a Protestant minister, and having members of the congregation in for tea had been a daily routine. The boy Hawes, for reasons best known to his father, had been included in the daily congregational tea-drinking visits. The tea, hefty, hot and hearty, had not stunted his growth at all. The man Hawes stood six feet two inches in his stocking feet, a redheaded giant who weighed in at a hundred and ninety pounds.

"She looked at me with these big blue eyes set in a face made for a doll," Parker said, "and she batted her eyelashes at me and said, 'I'm in a hurry. If you're going to give me the goddamn ticket, give it to me!'"

"Wow!" Hawes said.

"So I asked her what the hurry was, and she said she had to be on stage in five minutes flat."

"What kind of stage? One of the burly houses?"

"No, no, she was a dancer in a muscial comedy. A big hit, too. And it was just about eight-thirty, and she was breaking her neck to catch the curtain. So I pulled out my fountain pen and my pad, and she said, 'Or would you prefer two tickets to the biggest hit in town?' and she started digging into her purse, those bubs about to spill out of that tiny little bra and stop traffic away the hell up to the Aquarium."

"So how was the show?" Carella asked.

"I didn't take the tickets."

"Why not?"

"Because this way I had a private show of my own. It took me twenty minutes to write that ticket, and all that time she was squirming and wiggling on the front seat with those gorgeous pineapples ready to pop. Man, what an experience!"

"You're not only mean," Carella said, "you're also horny."

"That I am," Parker admitted proudly.

"I caught a guy once on Freeman Lewis Boulevard," Carella said. "He was doing eighty miles an hour. I had to put on the siren before he'd stop. I got out of the squad car and was walking over to his car when the door popped open, and he leaped out and started running toward me."

"A hood?" Hawes asked.

"No, but that's just what I thought. I figured I'd stumbled on a guy who was running from the law. I expected him to pull a gun any minute."

"What *did* he do?"

"He came up to me hopping up and down, first one leg, then the other. He said he knew he was speeding, but he'd just had an acute attack of diarrhea, and he had to find a gas station with a men's room in a hurry."

Parker burst out laughing. "Oh, brother, that takes it," he said.

"Did you let him go?" Hawes asked.

"Hell, no. I just wrote the ticket in a hurry, that's all."

"I'll tell you one I let go," Hawes said. "This was when I was a patrolman with the 30th. The guy was clipping along like a madman, and when I stopped him he just looked at me and said, 'You going to give me a ticket?' So I looked right back at him and said, 'Damn right, I'm going to give you a ticket.' He stared at me for a long time, just nodding his head. Then he said, 'That's it, then. You give me a ticket, and I'll kill myself.'"

"What the hell did he mean?"

"That's just what I said. I said, 'What do you mean, mister?' But he just kept staring at me, and he didn't say another word, just kept staring and nodding his head, over and over again, as if this ticket was the last straw, do you know what I mean? I had the feeling that this had just be one of those days where everything in the world had gone wrong for him, and I knew—I just knew as sure as I was standing there—that if I slapped a summons on him, he would actually go home and turn on the gas or jump out the window or slit his throat. I just knew it. I could just sense it about the guy."

"So you let him go. The Good Samaritan."

"Yeah, yeah, Samaritan," Hawes said. "You should have seen that guy's eyes. You'd have known he wasn't kidding."

"I had a woman once," Kling, the youngest of the detectives started, and Patrolman Dick Genero burst into the squadron carrying the small, blue overnight bag. One look at his eyes, and anyone would have known he wasn't kidding. He carried the bag in his right hand, far away from his body, as if afraid to be contaminated by it. He pushed his way through the gate in the slatted railing which separated the squadroom from the corridor outside, went directly to Parker's desk, and plunked the bag down in the middle of it with a finality that indicated he had done his duty and was now glad to be rid of it.

"What have you got, Dick?" Hawes asked.

Genero could not speak. His face was white, his eyes were wide. He swallowed several times, but no words came from his mouth. He kept shaking his head and pointing at the bag. Hawes stared at the bag in puzzlement, and then began to unzip it. Genero turned away. He seemed ready to vomit momentarily.

Hawes looked into the bag and said, "Oh, Jesus, where'd you get this?"

"What is it?" Kling asked.

"Oh, Jesus," Hawes said. "What a goddamn thing. Get it out of here. Jesus, get it out of the squadroom. I'll call the morgue." The rugged planes of his face were twisted in pain. He could not looked into the bag again. "I'll call the morgue," he said again. "Jesus, get it out of here. Take it downstairs. Get it out of here."

Carella picked up the bag and started out of the room.

He did not look into it. He did not have to.

He had been a cop for a long time now, and he knew instantly from the expression on Hawes's face that the bag must contain a segment of a human body.

Three

NOW THAT'S PRETTY DAMN DISGUSTING.

But let's get something straight. Death *is* pretty damn disgusting, and there are no two ways about it. If you are one of those people who like motion pictures where a man fires a gun and a small spurt of dust explodes on the victim's chest—just a small spurt of dust, no blood—then police work is not the line for you. Similarly, if you are one of those people who believe that corpses look "just like they're sleeping," it is fortunate you are not a cop. If you are a cop, you know that death is seldom pretty, that it is in fact the ugliest and most frightening event that can over take a human being.

If you are a cop, you have seen death at its ugliest because you have seen it as the result of violent upheaval. You have, more than likely, puked more than once at the things you have seen. You have, more than likely, trembled with fear, because death has a terrifying way of reminding the strongest human that his flesh can bleed and his bones can break. If you are a cop, you will never get used to the sight of a corpse or a part of a corpse—no matter how long you deal with them, no matter how strong you are, no matter how tough you become.

There is nothing reassuring about the sight of a man who has been worked over with a hatchet. The skull, a formidable piece of bone, assuming the characteristics of a melon, the parallel wounds, the criss-crossing wounds, the bleeding ugly wounds covering the head and the face and the neck, the windpipe exposed and raw, throbbing with color so bright, but throbbing only with color because life is gone, life has fled beneath the battering rigidity of an impersonal hatchet blade; there is nothing reassuring.

There is nothing beautiful about the post-mortem decomposition of a body, man or woman, child or adult, the gas formation, the discoloration of head and trunk tissues, the separation of epidermis, the staining of veins, the protrusion of tongue, decomposed liquefied fat soaking through the skin resulting in large yellow-stained areas; there is nothing beautiful.

There is nothing tender about bullet wounds, the smeared and lacerated flesh of contact wounds, the subcutaneous explosion of gases, the tissues seared and blackened by flame and smoke, the embedded powder grains, the gaping holes in the flesh; there is nothing tender.

If you are a cop, you learn that death is ugly, and frightening, and disgusting. If you are a cop, you learn to deal with what is ugly, frightening and disgusting or you quit the force.

The object in the overnight bag was a human hand, ugly, frightening and disgusting.

The man who received it at the morgue was an assistant medical examiner named Paul Blaney, a short man with a scraggly black mustache and violet eyes. Blaney didn't particularly enjoy handling the remains of dead people, and he often wondered why he—the junior member on the medical examiner's staff—was invariably given the most particularly obnoxious stiffs to examine, those who had been in automobile accidents, or fires, or whose remains had been chewed to ribbons by marauding rats. But he knew that he had a job to do. And that job was—given a human hand which has been severed at the wrist from the remainder of the body, how can I determine the race, sex, age, probable height and probable weight of the person to whom it belonged?

That was the job.

With a maximum of dispatch, and a minimum of emotional involvement, Blaney set to work.

Fortunately, the hand was still covered with skin. A lot of bodies he received simply weren't. And so it was quite simple to determine the race of the person to whom the

hand had belonged. Blaney determined that race rather
quickly, and then jotted the information on a slip of paper.

RACE: White.

Sex was another thing again. It was simple to identify
the sex of an individual if the examiner was presented with
remains of the breasts or sexual organs, but all Blaney had
was a hand. Period. Just a hand. In general, Blaney knew,
the female of the species usually had less body hair than
the male, more delicate extremities, more subcutaneous fat
and less musculature. Her bones, too, were smaller and
lighter, with thinner shafts and wider medullary spaces.

The hand on the autopsy table was a huge one. It measured twenty-five centimeters from the tip of the middle finger to the base of the severed wrist, and that came to something more than nine and a half inches when translated into
laymen's English. Blaney could not conceive of such a
hand having belonged to a woman, unless she were a mas-
seuse or a female wrestler. And even granting such exotic
occupations, the likelihood was remote. He had, nonetheless, made errors in determining the sex of a victim from
sex-unrelated parts in the past, and he did not wish to
make such an error now.

The hand was covered with thick, black, curling hair,
another fact which seemed to point toward a male identification; but Blaney carried the examination to its conclusion, measuring the bone shafts, studying the medullary
spaces, and jotting down his estimate at last.

SEX: Male.

Well, we're getting someplace, he thought. We now
know that this gruesome and severed member of a human
body once belonged to a white male. Wiping his forehead
with a towel, he got back to work again.

A microscopic examination of the hand's skin told Blaney that there had been no loss of elasticity due to the de-
crease of elastic fibers in the dermis. Since he was making
his microscopic examination in an effort to determine the
victim's age, he automatically chalked off the possibility of
the man's having been a very old one. He knew, further,
that he was not likely to get anything more from a closer
examination of the skin. The changes in skin throughout

the growth and decline of a human being very seldom provide accurate criteria of age. And so he turned to the bones.

The hand had been severed slightly above the wrist so that portions of the radius and ulna, the twin bones which run from the wrist to the elbow, were still attached to the hand. Moreover, Blaney had all the various bones of the hand itself to examine: the carpus, the metacarpal, the phalanx.

He mused, as he worked, that the average layman would —just about now—begin to consider all of his devious machinations as scientific mumbo jumbo, the aimless meanderings of a pseudo-wizard. Well, he thought, the hell with the average layman. I know damn well that the ossification centers of bones go through a sequence of growth and fusion, and that this growth and fusion takes place at certain age levels. I know further that by studying these bones, I can come pretty close to estimating the age of this dead white male, and that is just what I am going to do, average layman be damned.

The entire examination which Blaney conducted on the bones took close to three hours. His notes included such esoteric terms as "proximal epiphysial muscle" and "os magnum" and "multangulum majus" and the like. His final note simply read:

AGE: 18-24.

When it came to the probable height and weight of the victim, Blaney threw up his hands in despair. If he had been presented with a femur, a humerus, or a radius in its entirety, he would have measured any one of them in centimeters from joint surface to joint surface with the cartilage in place, and then made an attempt at calculating the height using Pearson's formula. For the radius, if he'd had a whole one and not just a portion of one, the table would have read like this:

MALE	FEMALE
86.465 plus 3.271 times length of radius.	82.189 plus 3.343 times length of radius.

Then, to arrive at an estimate of the height of the *living* body, he'd have subtracted 1.5 centimeters from the final result for a male, and 2 centimeters for a female.

Unfortunately, he didn't have a whole radius, so he didn't even make an attempt. And although the hand gave him a good knowledge of the size of the victim's bones, he could not make a guess at the weight of the victim without a knowledge of the muscular development and the adipose tissue, so he quit. He wrapped the hand and tagged it for delivery to Lieutenant Samuel G. Grossman at the Police Laboratory. Grossman, he knew, would perform an iso-reaction test on a blood specimen in order to determine the blood group. And Grossman would undoubtedly try to get fingerprint impressions from the severed hand. In this respect, Blaney was positively certain that Grossman would fail. Each finger tip had been neatly sliced away from the rest of the hand by the unknown assailant. A magician couldn't have got a set of prints from that hand, and Grossman was no magician.

So Blaney shipped off the hand, and he concluded his notes; and what he finally transmitted to the bulls of the 87th was this:

RACE: White.

SEX: Male.

AGE: 18-24.

The boys had to take it from there.

Four

DETECTIVE STEVE CARELLA was the first of the boys to take it from there.

He took it early the next morning. Sitting at his desk near the grilled squadroom windows, watching the rain ooze along the glass panes, he dialed Blaney's office and waited.

"Dr. Blaney," a voice on the other end of the wire said.

"Blaney, this is Carella up at the 87th."

"Hello," Blaney said.

"I've got your report on that hand, Blaney."

"Yeah? What's wrong with it?" Blaney asked, immediately on the defensive.

"Nothing at all," Carella said. "In fact, it's very helpful."

"Well, I'm glad to hear that," Blaney said. "It's very rare that anyone in the goddamn department admits a medical examination was helpful."

"We feel differently here at the 87th," Carella said smoothly. "We've always relied very heavily upon information provided by the medical examiner's office."

"Well, I'm certainly glad to hear that," Blaney said. "A man works here with stiffs all day long, he begins to have his doubts. It's no fun cutting up dead bodies, you know."

"You fellows do a wonderful job," Carella said.

"Well, thank you."

"I mean it," Carella said fervently. "There isn't much glory in what you fellows do, but you can bet your life it's appreciated."

"Well, thank you. Thank you."

"I wish I had a nickel for every case you fellows made

easier for us to crack," Carella said, more fervently this time, almost carried away by himself.

"Well, gosh, thanks. What can I do for you, Carella?"

"Your report was an excellent one," Carella said, "and very helpful, too. But there was just one thing."

"Yes?"

"I wonder if you can tell me anything about the person who did the job."

"Did the job?"

"Yes. Your report told us a lot about the victim, and that's excellent . . ."

"Yes?"

"Yes, and very helpful. But what about the perpetrator?"

"The perpetrator?"

"Yes, the man or woman who did the surgery."

"Oh. Oh, yes, of course," Blaney said. "You know, after you've been examining corpses for a while, you forget that someone was responsible for the corpse, do you know what I mean? It becomes . . . well, sort of a mathematical problem."

"I can understand that," Carella said. "But about the person responsible for this particular corpse, could you tell anything from the surgery?"

"Well, the hand was severed slightly above the wrist."

"Could you tell what kind of a tool was used?"

"Either a meat cleaver or a hatchet, I would say. Or something similar."

"Was it a clean job?"

"Fairly. Whoever did it had to hack through those bones. But there were no hesitation cuts anywhere on the hand, so the person who severed it from the body was probably determined and sure."

"Skillful?"

"How do you mean?"

"Well, would you say the person had any knowledge of anatomy?"

"I wouldn't think so," Blaney answered. "The logical place for the cut would have been at the wrist itself, where the radius and ulna terminate. That certainly would have been easier than hacking through those bones. No, I would discount anyone with a real knowledge of anatomy. In fact, I can't understand why the hand was dismembered, can you?"

"I don't think I follow you, Blaney?"

"You've seen dismemberment cases before, Carella. We usually find the head, and then the trunk, and then the four extremities. But if a person is going to cut off an arm, why then cut off the hand? Do you know what I mean? It's an added piece of work that doesn't accomplish very much."

"Yeah, I see," Carella said.

"Most bodies are dismembered or mutilated because the criminal is attempting to avoid identification of the body. That's why the fingertips of that hand were mutilated."

"Of course."

"And sometimes your killer will cut up the body to make disposal easier. But cutting off a hand at the wrist? How would that serve either purpose?"

"I don't know," Carella said. "In any case, we're not dealing with a surgeon or a doctor here, is that right?"

"I would say not."

"How about a butcher?"

"Maybe. The bones were severed with considerable force. That might imply a man familiar with his tools. the fingertips were neatly sliced."

"Okay, Blaney, thanks a lot."

"Any time," Blaney said happily, and hung up.

Carella thought for a moment about dismembered bodies. There was suddenly a very sour taste in his mouth. He went into the Clerical Office and asked Miscolo to make a pot of coffee.

In Captain Frick's office downstairs, a patrolman named Richard Genero was on the carpet. Frick, who was technically in command of the entire precinct—his command, actually, very rarely intruded upon the activities of the detective squad—was not a very imaginative man, nor in truth a very intelligent one. He liked being a policeman, he supposed, but he would rather have been a movie star. Movie stars got to meet glamorous women. Police captains only got to bawl out patrolmen.

"Am I to understand, Genero," he said, "that you don't know whether the person who left this bag on the sidewalk was a man or a woman, is that what I am made to understand, Genero?"

"Yes, sir," Genero said.

"You can't tell a man from a woman, Genero?"

"No, sir. I mean, yes, sir, I can sir, but it was raining."

"So?"

"And this person's face was covered. By an umbrella, sir."

"Was this person wearing a dress?"

"No, sir."

"A skirt?"

"No, sir."

"Pants?"

"Do you mean trousers, sir?"

"Yes, of course I mean trousers!" Frick shouted.

"Well, sir, yes, sir. That is, they could have been slacks. Like women wear, sir. Or they could have been trousers. Like men wear, sir."

"And what did you do when you saw the bag on the sidewalk?"

"I yelled after the bus, sir."

"And then what?"

"Then I opened the bag."

"And when you saw what was inside it?"

"I . . . I guess I got a little confused, sir."

"Did you go after the bus?"

"N . . . n . . . no, sir."

"Are you aware that there was another bus stop three blocks away?"

"No, sir."

"There was, Genero. Are you aware that you could have hailed a passing car, and caught that bus, and boarded it, and arrested the person who left this bag on the sidewalk? Are you aware of that, Genero?"

"Yes, sir. I mean, I wasn't aware of it at the time, sir. I am now, sir."

"And saved us the trouble of sending this bag to the laboratory, or of having the detective division trot all the way out to International Airport?"

"Yes, sir."

"Or of trying to find the other pieces of that body, of hoping we can identify the body *after* we have all the pieces, are you aware of all this, Genero?"

"Yes, sir."

"Then how can you be so goddamn stupid, Genero?"

"I don't know, sir."

"We contacted the bus company," Frick said. "The bus that passed that corner at two-thirty—was that the time, Genero?"

"Yes, sir."

"—at two-thirty was bus number 8112. We talked to the driver. He doesn't remember anyone in black boarding the bus at that corner, man or woman."

"There was a person, sir. I saw him. Or her, sir."

"No one's doubting your word, Genero. A bus driver can't be expected to remember everyone who gets on and off his goddamn bus. In any case, Genero, we're right back where we started. And all because you didn't think. Why didn't you think, Genero?"

"I don't know, sir. I was too shocked, I guess."

"Boy, there are times I wish I was a movie star or something," Frick said. "All right, get out. Look alive, Genero. Keep on your goddamn toes."

"Yes, sir."

"Go on, get out."

"Yes, sir." Genero saluted and left the captain's office hurriedly, thanking his lucky stars that no one had discovered he'd had two glasses of wine in Max Mandel's shop just before finding the bag. Frick sat at his desk and sighed heavily. Then he buzzed Lieutenant Byrnes upstairs and told him he could deliver the bag to the lab whenever he wanted to. Byrnes said he would send a man down for it at once.

The photograph of the bag lay on Nelson Piat's desk. "Yes, that's one of our bags, all right," he said. "Nice photograph, too. Did you take the photograph?"

"Me, personally, do you mean?" Detective Meyer Meyer asked.

"Yes."

"No. A police photographer took it."

"Well, it's our bag, all right," Piat said. He leaned back in his leather-covered swivel chair, dangerously close to the huge sheet of glass that formed one wall of his office. The office was on the fourth floor of the Administration Building at International Airport, overlooking the runway. The runway now was drenched with lashing curtains of rain that swept its slick surface. "Damn rain," Piat said. "Bad for our operation."

"Can't you fly when it rains?" Meyer asked.

"Oh, *we* can fly all right. *We* can fly in almost everything. But will the *people* fly, that's the question. The minute it begins raining, we get more damn cancellations than you can shake a stick at. Afraid. They're all afraid." Piat shook his head and studied the photo of the bag again. It was an $8\frac{1}{2} \times 11$ glossy print. The bag had been photographed against a white backdrop. It was an excellent picture, the company's name and slogan leaping out of the print as if they were molded in neon. "Well, what about this bag, gentlemen?" Piat said. "Did some burglar use it for his tools or something?" He chuckled at his own little joke and looked first to Kling and then to Meyer.

Kling answered for both of them. "Well, not exactly, sir," he said. "Some murderer used it for part of a corpse."

"Part of a . . . ? Oh. I see. Well, that's not too good. Bad for our operation." He paused. "Or is it?" He paused again, calculating. "Will this case be getting into the newspapers?"

"I doubt it," Meyer said. "It's a little too gory for the public, and so far it doesn't contain either a rape or a pretty girl in bloomers. It would make dull copy."

"I was thinking . . . you know . . . a photo of the bag

on the front pages of a mass circulation newspaper, that
might not be bad for our operation. Hell, you can't buy
that kind of advertising space, now can you? It might be
very good for our operation, who knows?"

"Yes, sir," Meyer said patiently.

If there was one virtue Meyer Meyer possessed, that
virtue was patience. And it was, in a sense, a virtue he
was born with or, at the very least, a virtue he was
named with. Meyer's father, you see, was something of a
practical joker, the kind of man who delighted in telling
kosher dinner guests during the middle of a meat meal
that they were eating off the dairy dishes. Oh, yes, he
was a gasser, all right. Well, when this gasser was well
past the age when changing diapers or wiping runny
noses was a possibility, when his wife had in fact experienced that remarkable female phenomenon euphemisti-
cally known as change of life, they were both somewhat
taken aback to learn that she was pregnant.

This was a surprising turn of events indeed, the practical joke supreme upon the king of the jesters. Meyer's
father fretted, pouted and sulked about it. His jokes suf-
fered while he planned his revenge against the vagaries
of nature and birth control. The baby was born, a
bouncing, blue-eyed boy delivered by a midwife and
weighing in at seven pounds six ounces. And then Meyer's pop delivered the final hilarious thrust. The baby's
first name would be Meyer, he decreed, and this handle
when coupled with the family name would give the boy
a title like a ditto mark: Meyer Meyer.

Well, that's pretty funny. Meyer's old man didn't stop
laughing for a week after the briss. Meyer, on the other
hand, found it difficult to laugh through bleeding lips.
The family was, you understand, practicing Orthodox
Judaism and they lived in a neighborhood which housed
a large Gentile population, and if the kids in the neighborhood needed another reason besides Meyer's Jewish-
ness for beating him up every day of the week, his name
provided that reason. "Meyer Meyer, Jew on fire!" the
kids would chant, and POW! Meyer got it in the kisser.

Over the years, he learned that it was impossible to

fight twelve guys at once, but that it was sometimes possible to talk this even dozen out of administering a beating. Patiently, he talked. Sometimes it worked. Sometimes it didn't. But patience became a way of life. And patience is a virtue, we will all admit. But if Meyer Meyer had not been forced to sublimate, if he had for example just once, just once when he was a growing boy been called Charlie or Frank or Sam and been allowed to stand up against one other kid, not a dozen or more, and bash that kid squarely on the nose, well perhaps, just perhaps, Meyer Meyer would not have been completely bald at the tender age of thirty-seven.

On the other hand, who would have been so cruel as to deprive an aging comedian of a small practical joke?

Patiently, Meyer Meyer said, "How are these bags distributed, Mr. Piat?"

"Distributed? Well, they're not exactly distributed. That is to say, they are given to people who fly with our airline. It's good for the operation."

"These bags are given to every one of your passengers, is that correct?"

"No, not exactly. We have several types of flights, you see."

"Yes?"

"Yes. We have our Luxury flight which gives more space between the seats, a big big twenty inches to stretch those legs in, and drinks en route, and a choice of several dinners, and special baggage accommodations —in short, the finest service our operation can offer."

"Yes?"

"Yes. And then we have our First-Class flight which offers the same accommodations and the same seating arrangement except that drinks are not provided—you can buy them, of course, if you desire—and there is only one item on the dinner menu, usually roast beef, or ham, or something of the sort."

"I see."

"And then we have our Tourist flight."

"Tourist flight, yes," Meyer said.

"Our Tourist flight which gives only sixteen inches of

leg room, but the same accommodations otherwise, including the same dinner as on the First-Class flight."

"I see. And this bag . . ."

"And then there is our Economy flight, same amount of leg room, but there are three seats on one side of the aisle, instead of two, and the dinner is not a hot meal, just sandwiches and, of course, no drinks."

"And of all these flights, which . . ."

"Then there's our Thrift flight which is not too comfortable, I'm afraid, that is to say not as comfortable as the other flights, but certainly comfortable enough, with only twelve inches of leg room, and . . ."

"Is that the last flight?" Meyer asked patiently.

"We're now working on one called the Piggy Bank flight, which will be even less expensive. What we're trying to do, you see, we're trying to put our operation within reach of people who wouldn't ordinarily consider flying, who would take the old-fashioned means of conveyance, like trains, or cars, or boats. Our operation . . ."

"Who gets the bags?" Kling asked impatiently.

"What? Oh, yes, the bags. We give them to all passengers on the Luxury or First-Class flights."

"*All* passengers?"

"All."

"And when did you start doing this?"

"At least six years ago," Piat said.

"Then anyone who rode either Luxury or First-Class in the past six years could conceivably have one of these bags, is that right?" Meyer asked.

"That is correct."

"And how many people would you say . . ."

"Oh, thousands and thousands and thousands," Piat said. "You must remember, Detective Meyer . . ."

"Yes?"

"We circle the globe."

"Yes," Meyer said. "Forgive me. With all those flights zooming around, I guess I lost sight of the destinations."

"Is there any possibility this might get into the newspapers?"

"There's always a possibility," Meyer said, rising.

"If it does, would you contact me? I mean, if you know about it beforehand. I'd like to get our promotion department to work."

"Sure thing," Meyer said. "Thank you for your time, Mr. Piat."

"Not at all," Piat said, shaking hands with Meyer and Kling. "Not at all." As they walked across the room to the door, he turned to the huge window and looked out over the rain-soaked runway. "Damn rain," he said.

Five

FRIDAY MORNING.

Rain.

When he was a kid, he used to walk six blocks to the library in the rain, wearing a mackinaw with the collar turned up, and feeling very much like Abraham Lincoln. Once there, he would sit in the warmth of the wood-paneled reading room, feeling strangely and richly rewarded while he read and the rain whispered against the streets outside.

And sometimes, at the beach, it would begin raining suddenly, the clouds sweeping in over the ocean like black horsemen in a clanging cavalry charge, the lightning scraping the sky like angry scimitar slashes. The girls would grab for sweaters and beach bags, and someone would reach for the portable record player and the stack of 45-rpms's, and the boys would hold the blanket overhead like a canopy while they all ran to the safety of the boardwalk restaurant. They would stand there and look out at the rain-swept beach, the twisted, lipsticked straws in deserted Coca Cola bottles, and there was comfort to the gloom somehow.

In Korea, Bert Kling learned about a different kind of rain. He learned about a rain that was cruel and driving and bitter, a rain that turned the earth to a sticky clinging mud that halted machines and men. He learned what it was to be constantly wet and cold. And ever since Korea, he had not liked the rain.

He did not like it on that late Friday morning, either.

He had started the day by paying a visit to the Missing Persons Bureau and renewing his acquaintance there with Detectives Ambrose and Bartholdi.

"Well, well, look who is here," Bartholdi had said.

"The Sun God of the 87th," Ambrose added.

"The Blond Wonder himself."

"In person," Kling said dryly.

"What can we do for you today, Detective Kling?"

"Who did you lose this week, Detective Kling?"

"We're looking for a white male between the ages of eighteen and twenty-four," Kling said.

"Did you hear that, Romeo?" Ambrose said to Bartholdi.

"I heard it, Mike," Bartholdi answered.

"That is an awful lot to go on. Now how many white males between the ages of eighteen and twenty-four do you suppose we have records on?"

"At a conservative estimate," Bartholdi answered, "I would say approximately six thousand seven hundred and twenty-three."

"Not counting the ones we ain't had time to file yet."

"With bulls from all over the city popping in here at every hour of the day, we don't get much time to do filing, Detective Kling."

"That's a shame," Kling said dryly. He wished he could shake the feeling he constantly experienced in the presence of older cops who'd been on the force longer than he. He knew he was a young detective and a new detective, but he resented the automatic assumption that because of his age and inexperience he must, ipso facto, be an inept detective. He did not consider himself inept. In fact, he thought of himself as being a pretty good cop, Romeo and Mike be damned.

"Can I look through the files?" he asked.

"But of course!" Bartholdi said enthusiastically. "That's why they're here! So that every dirty-fingered cop in the city can pore over them. Ain't that right, Mike?"

"Why, certainly. How else would we keep busy? If we

didn't have dog-eared record cards to retype, we might have to go outside on a lousy day like this. We might have to actually use a gun now and then."

"We prefer leaving the gunplay to you younger, more agile fellows, Kling."

"To the heroes," Ambrose said.

"Yeah," Kling answered, and he searched for a more devastating reply, but none came to mind.

"Be careful with our cards," Bartholdi cautioned. "Did you wash your hands this morning?"

"I washed them," Kling said.

"Good. Obey the sign." He pointed to the large placard resting atop the green filing cabinets.

SHUFFLE THEM, JUGGLE THEM, MAUL THEM, CARESS THEM—BUT LEAVE THEM THE WAY YOU FOUND THEM!

"Got it?" Ambrose asked.

"I've been here before," Kling said. "You ought to change your sign. It gets kind of dull the hundredth time around."

"It ain't there for entertainment," Bartholdi said. "It's there for information."

"Take care of the cards," Ambrose said. "If you get bored, look up a dame named Barbara Cesare, also known as Bubbles Caesar. She was reported missing in February. That's over there near the window. She was a stripper in Kansas City, and she came here to work some of our own clubs. There are some very fine art photos in her folder."

"He is just a boy, Mike," Bartholdi said. "You shouldn't call his attention to matters like that."

"Forgive me, Romeo," Ambrose said. "You're right. Forget I mentioned Bubbles Caesar, Kling. Forget all about them lovely pictures in the February file over there near the window. You hear?"

"I'll forget all about her," Kling said.

"We got typing to do," Bartholdi said, opening the door. "Have fun."

"That's Caesar," Ambrose said as he went out. "C-A-E-S-A-R."

"Bubbles," Bartholdi said, and he closed the door behind him.

Kling, of course, did not have to look through 6,723 missing persons cards. If anything, the haphazard estimate given by Bartholdi was somewhat exaggerated. Actually, some 2,500 persons were reported missing annually in the city for which Kling worked. If this was broken down on a monthly basis, perhaps a little more than 200 people per month found their way into the files of the Missing Persons Bureau. The peak months for disappearances are May and September, but Kling, fortunately, was not particularly concerned with those months. He restricted himself to scouring the files covering January, February, and the early part of March, and so he didn't have very many folders to wade through.

The job, nonetheless, did get somewhat boring, and he did—since he was studying the February file, anyway—take a peek into the folder of the missing exotic dancer, Bubbles Caesar. He had to admit, after studying the several photos of her in the folder, that whoever had named this performer had a decided knack for the *mot juste*. Looking at the pictures of the stripper made him think of Claire Townsend, and thinking of Claire made him wish it was tonight instead of this morning.

He lighted another cigarette, ruefully put away Miss Caesar's folder, and got back to work again.

By eleven o'clock that morning, he had turned up only two possible nominations for the Missing Persons Award. He went down the hall and had both sheets photostated. Bartholdi, who did the job for him, seemed to be in a more serious frame of mind now.

"These what you were looking for, kid?" he asked.

"Well, they're only possibilities. We'll see how they turn out."

"What's the case, anyway?" Bartholdi asked.

"One of our patrolmen found a severed hand in a bag."

"Psssssss," Bartholdi said and he pulled a face.

"Yeah. Right in the street. Near a bus stop."

"Psssssss," Bartholdi said again.

"Yeah."

"A man or a woman? The hand, I mean."

"A man," Kling said.

"What kind of a bag? A shopping bag?"

"No, no," Kling said. "An airlines bag. You know these bags they give out? These little blue ones? This one came from an outfit called Circle Airlines."

"A high-flying killer, huh?" Bartholdi said. "Well, here are the stats, kid. Good luck with them."

"Thanks," Kling said. He took the proffered manila envelope and went down the corridor to a phone booth. He dialed Frederick 7-8024 and asked to talk to Steve Carella.

"Some weather, huh?" Carella said.

"The end," Kling answered. "Listen, I dug up two possibles from the files here. Thought I'd hit the first before lunch. You want to come with me?"

"Sure," Carella said. "Where shall I meet you?"

"Well, the first guy is a merchant seaman, vanished on February 14, Valentine's Day. His wife reported him missing. She lives on Detavoner, near South Eleventh."

"Meet you on the corner there?"

"Fine," Kling said. "Were there any calls for me?"

"Claire called."

"Yeah?"

'Said you should call her back as soon as you got a chance."

"Oh? Okay, thanks," Kling said. "I'll see you in about a half-hour, okay?"

"Right. Stay out of the rain." And he hung up.

Now, standing in the rain on what was probably the most exposed corner in the entire city, Kling tried to crawl deep into his trench coat, tried to form an airtight, watertight seal where his hands were thrust deep into his coat pockets, tried to pull in his neck like a turtle, but nothing worked against the goddamn rain, everything was wet and cold and clammy, and where the hell was Carella?

I wish I wore a hat, he thought. I wish I were that kind of American advertising executive who could feel comfortable in a hat.

Hatless, his blond hair soaked and plastered to his skull, Kling stood on the street corner observing:

a) the open parking lot on one corner.

b) the skycraper under construction on the opposite corner.

c) the fenced-in park on the third corner.

d) the blank wall of a warehouse on the fourth corner.

No canopies under which to stand. No doorways into which a man could duck. Nothing but the wide open spaces of Isola and the rain driving across those spaces like a Cossack charge in an Italian-made spectacle. Damn you, Carella, where are you?

Aw, come on, Steve, he thought. Have a heart.

The unmarked police sedan pulled to the curb. A sign on the lamppost read NO PARKING OR STANDING 8:00 A.M. TO 6:00 P.M. Carella parked the car and got out.

"Hi," he said. "Been waiting long?"

"What the hell kept you?" Kling wanted to know.

"Grossman called from the lab just as I was leaving."

"Yeah? So what . . . ?"

"He's working on both the hand and the bag now, says he'll have a report for us sometime tomorrow."

"Will he get any prints from the hand?"

"He doubts it. The finger tips are cut to ribbons. Listen, can't we discuss this over a cup of coffee? Must we stand here in the rain? And I'd also like to take a look at that Missing Person sheet before we see this woman."

"I can use a cup of coffee," Kling said.

"Does she knew we're coming? The guy's wife?"

"No. You think I should have called?"

"No, better this way. Maybe we'll find her with a body in a trunk and a meat cleaver in her dainty fist."

"Sure. There's a diner in the middle of the block.

Let's get the coffee there. You can look over the sheet while I buzz Claire."

"Good," Carella said.

They walked to the diner, sat in one of the booths, and ordered two cups of coffee. While Kling went to call his fiancée, Carella sipped at his coffee and studied the report. He read it through once, and then he read it through a second time. This is what it said:

POLICE DEPARTMENT
REPORT OF MISSING PERSON

PCT. DISTRICT	2nd
CASE No.	B26-1143
M.P. Bur. No.	24A-1762
DATE OF THIS REPORT	2/16

SURNAME AKERVITCH

FIRST NAME, INITIALS EARL F.

ADDRESS 537 Detavoner Avenue

PROBABLE DESTINATION B. B. Fatven, Pier 6

LAST SEEN AT Home address

CAUSE OF ABSENCE ?

NATIVITY	SEX	AGE	DATE AND TIME SEEN	COLOR
U.S.A.	M	23	2/14 8:30 A.M.	White
			DATE AND TIME REPORTED	
			2/15 9:00 A.M.	

PHYSICAL — NOTE PECULIARITIES

HEIGHT	FT. 6 IN. 4½
WEIGHT	210
BUILD	Husky
COMPLEXION	Sallow
HAIR	Brown
EYES	Brown
GLASSES, TYPE	
MUSTACHE-BEARD	Brown, close-trimmed

CLOTHING—GIVE COLOR, FABRIC, STYLE, LABEL WHERE POSSIBLE

HEADGEAR	Watchcap, blue wool
OVERCOAT OR COAT	None
SUIT OR DRESS	
JACKET (BUSINESS)	Peajacket. Blue.
TROUSERS (DRESS)	Dungarees, blue, faded
SHIRT	White, cotton, long-sleeved, Manhattan label
GLOVES	
SCARF	
HOSE	Black socks, cotton dacron, Esquire

STRIKE OUT IRRELEVANT WORDS

MISCELLANEOUS INFORMATION

OCCUPATION OF SCHOOL	Fiper, B. B. Fatven
EVER SINCE?COUNTRY WHERE AND WHEN	Yes. March—Mar. 3/4/58
DRY CLEANER MARK	In jacket. Detavoner Cleaners. 601 Detavoner Avenue
LAUNDRY MARK	
PHOTO RECEIVED	Yes
PREVIOUSLY MISSING?	No
PUBLICITY DESIRED?	Yes
SOCIAL SECURITY NO.	119-16-1633

PRELIMINARY INVESTIGATION Ptlmn Ralph Clmnetar

DESK OFFICER Lt. E. Kool

TEETH	SHOES		TELEGRAPH BUREAU
No dental chart	Black, untrimmed		Sgt. E. Abrenoff
	HANDBAG		BUREAU OF INFORMATION
			Det. 1st/Gr D. Nicholson
SCARS	LUGGAGE		OTHERS
	Duffel bag, canvas, white, stenciled "K. F. ANDROVICH"		
	JEWELRY WORN		
	None		
DEFORMITIES			NOTIFICATION TO MISSING PERSONS BUR. BY
			Det./Lt. Franklin Canavan, 26 Dets.
	MONEY CARRIED		
	$30.00		RECEIVED AT MISSING PERSONS BUREAU BY
TATTOO MARKS "PEG" in Heart on left biceps	CHARACTERISTICS, HABITS, MANNERISMS Left eye. Stammers when excited. Very hot-tempered.	BELELAS ETC.	Det. Sean O'Rourke
			SQUAD ASSIGNED
			ASSIGNED 4h P. DET.
PHYSICAL CONDITION Good	MENTAL Good		Det. 2/Gr Jonah Fredericks
REPORTED BY Margaret Androvich	ADDRESS 657 Detavoner Avenue		TELEPHONE NO. IS 4-7381 RELATIONSHIP Wife

REMARKS

Androvich left his apartment at 657 Detavoner Avenue at 6:30 A.M. on February 14 apparently to board his ship, the SS Farren, where it was docked at Pier 6. He was scheduled to sail for South America at 8:00 A.M. that morning, and gave every indication of wanting to catch the ship. His wife noticed nothing strange about his behavior at breakfast, which they ate together in the apartment. At 7:45 A.M., the chief officer of the Farren called to inquire of Androvich's whereabouts. His wife told the officer that Androvich had left the apartment at 6:30. She did not report his absence to the police during the remainder of that day, because she was hopeful he would return by morning. This was the first time, except when on cruises, that he has been gone for any prolonged length of time.

Det. Jonah Fredericks
Signature of Assigned Detective

Lt. Samuel Barker
Commanding Officer

When Kling came back to the table, there was a smile
on his face.

"What's up?" Carella asked.

"Oh, nothing much. Claire's father left for New Jer-
sey this morning, that's all. Won't be back until Monday."

"Which gives you an empty apartment for the weekend, huh?" Carella said.

"Well, I wasn't thinking of anything like that," Kling
said.

"No, of course not."

"But it might be nice," Kling admitted.

"When are you going to marry that girl?"

"She wants to get her master's degree before we get
married."

"Why?"

"How do I know? She's insecure." Kling shrugged.
"She's psychotic. How do I know?"

"What does she want after the master's? A docto-
rate?"

"Maybe." Kling shrugged. "Listen, I ask her to marry
me every time I see her. She wants the master's. So what
can I do? I'm in love with her. Can I tell her to go to
hell?"

"I suppose not."

"Well, I can't." Kling paused. "I mean, what the hell,
Steve, if a girl wants an education, it's not my right to
say no, is it?"

"I guess not."

"Well, would you have said no to Teddy?"

"I don't think so."

"Well, there you are."

"Sure."

"I mean, what the hell else can I do, Steve? I either
wait for her, or I decide not to marry her, right?"

"Right," Carella said.

"And since I want to marry her, I have no choice. I
wait." He paused thoughtfully. "Jesus, I hope she isn't
one of those perennial schoolgirl types." He paused

again. "Well, there's nothing I can do about it. I'll just have to wait, that's all."

"That sounds like sound deduction."

"Sure. The only thing is . . . well, to be absolutely truthful with you, Steve, I'm afraid she'll get pregnant or something, and then we'll *have* to get married, do you know what I mean? And that'll be different than if we just got married because we felt like it. I mean, even though we love each other and all, it'd be different. Oh, Jesus, I don't know what to do."

"Just be careful, that's all," Carella said.

"Oh, I am. I mean, we are, we are. You want to know something, Steve?"

"What?"

"I wish I could keep my hands off her. You know, I wish we didn't have to . . . well, you know, my land-lady looks at me cockeyed every time I bring Claire upstairs. And then I have to rush her home because her father is the strictest guy who ever walked the earth. I'm surprised he's leaving her alone this weekend. But what I mean is . . . well, damnit, what the hell does she need that master's for, Steve? I mean, I wish I could leave her alone until we were married, but I just can't. I mean, all I have to do is be with her, and my mouth goes dry. Is it that way with . . . well, never mind, I didn't mean to get personal."

"It's that way," Carella said.

"Yeah," Kling said, and he nodded. He seemed lost in thought for a moment. Then he said, "I've got tomorrow off, but not Sunday. Do you think somebody would want to switch with me? Like for a Tuesday or something? I hate to break up the weekend."

"Where'd you plan to spend the weekend?" Carella asked.

"Well, you know . . ."

"*All* weekend?" Carella said, surprised.

"Well, you know . . ."

"Starting *tonight?*" he asked, astonished.

"Well, you know . . ."

"I'd give you my Sunday, but I'm afraid . . ."

"Will you?" Kling said, leaning forward.

". . . you'll be a wreck on Monday morning." Carella paused. "*All* weekend?" he asked again.

"Well, it isn't often the old man goes away. You know."

"Flaming Youth, where have you gone?" Carella said, shaking his head. "Sure, you can have my Sunday if the Skipper says okay."

"Thanks, Steve."

"Or did Teddy have something planned?" Carella asked himself.

"Now don't change your mind," Kling said anxiously.

"Okay, okay." He tapped the Missing Persons report with his forefinger. "What do you think?"

"He looks good, I would say. He's big enough, anyway. Six-four and weighs two-ten. That's no midget, Steve."

"And that hand belonged to a big man." Carella finished his coffee and said, "Come on, Lover Man, let's go see Mrs. Androvich."

As they rose, Kling said, "It's not that I'm a great lover or anything, Steve. It's just . . . well . . ."

"What?"

Kling grinned. "I *like* it," he said.

Six

MARGARET ANDROVICH WAS a nineteen-year-old blonde who, in the hands of our more skillful novelists, would have been described as willowy. That is to say, she was skinny. The diminutive "Meg" did not exactly apply to her because she was five feet seven and a half inches tall with all the cuddly softness of a steel cable. In the current fashion of naming particularly svelte women with particularly ugly names, "Maggie" would have been more appropriate than the "Meg" which Karl Androvich wore tattooed in a heart on his left arm. But Meg she was, all five feet seven and a half inches of her, and she greeted the detectives at the door with calm and assurance, ushered them into her living room, and asked them to sit.

They sat.

She was indeed skinny with that angular sort of femininity which is usually attributed to fashion models. She was not, at the moment, attired for the pages of *Vogue* Magazine. She was wearing a faded pink quilted robe and furry pink slippers which somehow seemed out of place on a girl so tall. Her face was as angular as her body, with high cheekbones and a mouth which looked pouting even without the benefit of lipstick. Her eyes were blue and large, dominating the narrow face. She spoke with a mild, barely discernible Southern accent. She carried about her the air of a person who knows she is about to be struck in the face with a closed fist but who bears the eventuality with calm expectation.

"Is this about Karl?" she asked gently.

"Yes, Mrs. Androvich," Carella answered.

"Have you heard anything? Is he all right?"

"No, nothing definite," Carella said.

"But something?"

"No, no. We just wanted to find out a little more about him, that's all."

"I see." She nodded vaguely. "Then you haven't heard anything about him."

"No, not really."

"I see." Again she nodded.

"Can you tell us what happened on the morning he left here?"

"Yes," she said. "He just left, that was all. There was nothing different between this time and all the other times he left to catch his ship. It was just the same. Only this time he didn't catch the ship." She shrugged. "And I haven't heard from him since." She shrugged again. "It's been almost a month now."

"How long have you been married, Mrs. Androvich?"

"To Karl? Six months."

"Had you been married before? I mean, is Karl your second husband?"

"No. He's my first husband. Only husband I ever had."

"Where did you meet him, Mrs. Androvich?"

"Atlanta."

"Six months ago?"

"Seven months ago, really."

"And you got married?"

"Yes."

"And you came to this city?"

"Yes."

"Where is your husband from originally?"

"Here. This city." She paused. "Do you like it here?"

"The city, do you mean?"

"Yes. Do you like it?"

"Well, I was born and raised here," Carella said. "Yes, I guess I like it."

"I don't," Meg said flatly.

"Well, that's what makes horse races, Mrs. Androvich,"

Carella said, and he tried a smile and then pulled it back quickly when he saw her face.

"Yes, that's what makes horse races, all right," she said. "I tried to tell Karl that I didn't like it here, that I wanted to go back to Atlanta. But he was born and raised here, too." She shrugged. "I guess it's different if you know the place. And with him gone so often, I'm alone a lot, and the streets confuse me. I mean, Atlanta isn't exactly a one-horse town, but it's small compared to here. I can never figure out how to *get* any place here. I'm always getting lost. I wander three blocks from the apartment, and I get lost. Would you like some coffee?"

"Well . . ."

"Have some coffee," Meg said. "You're not going to rush right off, are you? You all are the first two people I've had here in a long time."

"I think we can stay for some coffee," Carella said.

"It won't take but a minute. Would you excuse me, please?"

She went into the kitchen. Kling rose from where he was sitting and walked to the television set. A framed photograph of a man rested atop the receiver. He was studying the photo when Meg came back into the room.

"That's Karl," she said. "That's a nice picture. That's the one I sent to the Missing Persons Bureau." She paused. "They asked me for a picture, you know." She paused again. "Coffee won't take but a minute. I'm warming some rolls, too. You men must be half-froze, wandering about in that cold rain."

"That's very nice of you, Mrs. Androvich."

She smiled fleetingly. "Working man needs sustenance," she said, and the smile vanished.

"Mrs. Androvich, about that morning he left . . ."

"Yes. It was Valentine's Day." She paused. "There was a big box of candy on the kitchen table when I woke up. And flowers came later. While we were having breakfast."

"From Karl?"

"Yes. Yes, from Karl."

"While you were having breakfast?"

"Yes."

"But . . . didn't he leave the house at 6:30?"

"Yes."

"And flowers arrived before he left?"

"Yes."

"That's pretty early, isn't it?"

"I guess he made some sort of arrangement with the florist," Meg said. "To have them delivered so early." She paused. "They were roses. Two dozen red roses."

"I see," Carella said.

"Anything out of the ordinary happen during breakfast?" Kling asked.

"No. No, he was in a very cheerful frame of mind."

"But he wasn't always in a cheerful frame of mind, is that also right? You told someone earlier that he was very hot-tempered."

"Yes. I told that to Detective Fredericks. At the Missing Persons Bureau. Do you know him?"

"No, not personally."

"He's a very nice man."

"And you told Detective Fredericks that your husband stammers, is that right? And he has a slight tic in the right eye, is that correct?"

"The left eye."

"Yes, the left eye."

"That's correct."

"Is he a nervous person, would you say?"

"He's pretty tense, yes."

"Was he tense on that morning?"

"The morning he left, do you mean?"

"Yes. Was he tense or nervous then?"

"No. He was very calm."

"I see. And what did you do with the flowers when they arrived?"

"The flowers? I put them in a vase."

"On the table?"

"Yes."

"The breakfast table?"

"Yes."

"They were there while you ate breakfast?"

"Yes."

"Did he eat a good meal?"

"Yes."

"His appetite was all right?"

"It was fine. He was very hungry."

"And nothing seemed unusual or strange?"

"No." She turned her head toward the kitchen. "I think the coffee's perking," she said. "Will you excuse me, please?"

She went out of the room. Kling and Carella sat staring at each other. Outside, the rain slithered down the windowpane.

She came back into the living room carrying a tray with a coffeepot, three cups and saucers, and a dish of hot rolls. She put these down, studied the tray, and then said, "Butter. I forgot butter." In the doorway to the kitchen, she paused and said, "Would you all like some jam or something?"

"No, this is fine, thanks," Carella said.

"Would you pour?" she said, and she went out for the butter. From the kitchen, she called, "Did I bring out the cream?"

"No," Carella said.

"Or the sugar?"

"No."

They heard her rummaging in the kitchen. Carella poured coffee into the three cups. She came into the room again and put down the butter, the cream and the sugar.

"There," she said. "Do you take anything in yours, Detective—Carella, was it?"

"Yes, Carella. No thank you, I'll have it black."

"Detective Kling?"

"A little cream and one sugar, thank you."

"Help yourself to the rolls before they get cold," she said.

The detectives helped themselves. She sat opposite them, watching.

"Take your coffee, Mrs. Androvich," Carella said.

"Oh, yes. Thank you." She picked up her cup, put three spoonfuls of sugar into it, and sat stirring it idly.

"Do you think you'll find him?" she asked.

"We hope so."

"Do you think anything's happened to him?"

"That's hard to say, Mrs. Androvich."

"He was such a big man." She shrugged.

"*Was*, Mrs. Androvich?"

"Did I say 'was'? I guess I did. I guess I think of him as gone for good."

"Why should you think that?"

"I don't know."

"It sounds as if he was very much in love with you."

"Oh yes. Yes, he was." She paused. "Are the rolls all right?"

"Delicious," Carella said.

"Fine," Kling added.

"I get them delivered. I don't go out much. I'm here most of the time. Right here in this apartment."

"Why do you think your husband went off like that, Mrs. Androvich?"

"I don't know."

"You didn't quarrel or anything that morning, did you?"

"No. No, we didn't quarrel."

"I don't mean a real fight or anything," Carella said. "Just a quarrel, you know. Anyone who's married has a quarrel every now and then."

"Are you married, Detective Carella?"

"Yes, I am."

"Do you quarrel sometimes?"

"Yes."

"Karl and I didn't quarrel that morning," she said flatly.

"But you did quarrel sometimes?"

"Yes. About going back to Atlanta mostly. That was all. Just about going back to Atlanta. Because I don't like this city, you see."

"That's understandable," Carella said. "Not being familiar with it, and all. Have you ever been uptown?"

"Uptown where?"

"Culver Avenue? Hall Avenue?"

"Where the big department stores are?"

"No, I was thinking of a little further uptown. Near Grover Park."

"No. I don't know where Grover Park is."

"You've never been uptown?"

"Not that far uptown."

"Do you have a raincoat, Mrs. Androvich?"

"A what?"

"A raincoat."

"Yes, I do. Why?"

"What color is it, Mrs. Androvich?"

"My *raincoat*?"

"Yes."

"It's blue." She paused. "Why?"

"Do you have a black one?"

"No. Why?"

"Do you ever wear slacks?"

"Hardly ever."

"But sometimes you do wear slacks?"

"Only in the house sometimes. When I'm cleaning. I never wear them in the street. Where I was raised, in Atlanta, a girl wore dresses and skirts and pretty things."

"Do you have an umbrella, Mrs. Androvich?"

"Yes, I do."

"What color is it?"

"Red. I don't think I understand all this, Detective Carella."

"Mrs. Androvich, I wonder if we could see the raincoat and the umbrella."

"What for?"

"Well, we'd like to."

She stared at Carella and then turned her puzzled gaze on Kling. "All right," she said at last. "Would you come into the bedroom, please?" They followed her into the other room. "I haven't made the bed yet, you'll have to forgive the appearance of the house." She pulled the blanket up over the rumpled sheets as she passed the bed on the way to the closet. She threw open the closet door and said, "There's the raincoat. And there's the umbrella."

The raincoat was blue. The umbrella was red.

"Thank you," Carella said. "Do you have your meat delivered, too, Mrs. Androvich?"

"My what?"

"Meat. From the butcher."

"Yes, I do. Detective Carella, would you mind please telling me what this is all about? All these questions, you make it sound as if . . ."

"Well, it's just routine, Mrs. Andovich, that's all. Just trying to learn a little about your husband's habits, that's all."

"What's my raincoat and my umbrella got to do with Karl's habits?"

"Well, you know."

"No, I don't know."

"Do you own a meat cleaver, Mrs. Androvich?"

She stared at Carella a long time before answering. Then she said, "What's that got to do with Karl?"

Carella did not answer.

"Is Karl dead?" she said. "Is that it?"

He did not answer.

"Did someone use a meat cleaver on him? Is that it? Is that it?"

"We don't know, Mrs. Androvich."

"Do you think I did it? Is that what you're saying?"

"We have no knowledge whatever about your husband's whereabouts, Mrs. Androvich. Dead or alive. This is all routine."

"Routine, huh? What happened? Did someone wearing a raincoat and carrying an umbrella hit my husband with a cleaver? Is that what happened?"

"No, Mrs. Androvich. *Do* you own a meat cleaver?"

"Yes, I do," she said. "It's in the kitchen. Would you like to see it? Maybe you can find some of Karl's skull on it. Isn't that what you'd like to find?"

"This is just a routine investigation, Mrs. Androvich."

"Are all detectives as subtle as you?" she wanted to know.

"I'm sorry if I've upset you, Mrs. Androvich. May I see that cleaver? If it's not too much trouble."

"This way," she said coldly, and she led them out of the bedroom, through the living room, and into the kitchen. The cleaver was a small one, its cutting edge dull and nicked. "That's it," she said.

"I'd like to take this with me, if you don't mind," Carella said.

"Why?"

"What kind of candy did your husband bring you on Valentine's Day, Mrs. Androvich?"

"Nuts. Fruits. A mixed assortment."

"From where? Who made the candy?"

"I don't remember."

"Was it a large box?"

"A pound."

"But you called it a big box of candy when you first spoke of it. You said there was a big box of candy on the kitchen table when you woke up. Isn't that what you said?"

"Yes. It was in the shape of a heart. It looked big to me."

"But it was only a pound box of candy, is that right?"

"Yes."

"And the dozen red roses? When did they arrive?"

"At about six A.M."

"And you put them in a vase?"

"Yes."

"Do you have a vase big enough to hold a dozen roses?"

"Yes, of course I do. Karl was always bringing me flowers. So I bought a vase one day."

"Big enough to hold a dozen red roses, right?"

"Yes."

"They *were* red roses, a dozen of them?"

"Yes."

"No *white* ones? Just a dozen red roses?"

"Yes, yes, a dozen red roses. All red. And I put them in a vase."

"You said two dozen, Mrs. Androvich. When you first mentioned them, you said there were two dozen."

"What?"

"Two dozen."

"I . . ."

"Were there any flowers at all, Mrs. Androvich?"

"Yes, yes. Yes, there were flowers. I must have made a mistake. It was only a dozen. Not two dozen. I must have been thinking of something else."

"Was there candy, Mrs. Androvich?"

"Yes, of course there was candy."

"Yes, and you didn't quarrel at the breakfast table. Why didn't you report his absence until the next day?"

"Because I thought . . ."

"Had he ever wandered off before?"

"No, he . . ."

"Then this was rather unusual for him, wasn't it?"

"Yes, but . . ."

"Then why didn't you report it immediately?"

"I thought he'd come back."

"Or did you think he had reason for staying away?"

"What reason?"

"You tell me, Mrs. Androvich."

The room went silent.

"There was no reason," she said at last. "My husband loved me. There was a box of candy on the table in the morning. A heart. The florist delivered a dozen red roses at six o'clock. Karl kissed me goodbye and left. And I haven't seen him since."

"Give Mrs. Androvich a receipt for this meat cleaver, Bert," Carella said. "Thank you very much for the coffee and rolls. And for your time. You were very kind."

As they went out, she said, "He *is* dead, isn't he?"

Claire Townsend was easily as tall as Meg Androvich, but the similarity between the two girls ended there. Meg was skinny—or, if you prefer, willowy; Claire was richly endowed with flesh that padded the big bones of her body. Meg, in the fashion-model tradition, was flat-chested. Claire was not one of those overextended cow-like creatures, but she was rightfully proud of a bosom capable of filling a man's hand. Meg was a blue-eyed blonde. Claire's eyes were brown and her hair was as black as sin. Meg, in short, gave the impression of some-one living in the pallor of a hospital sickroom; Claire looked like a girl who would be at home on a sun-washed haystack.

There was one other difference.

Bert Kling was madly in love with Claire.

She kissed him the moment he entered the apartment. She was wearing black slacks and a wide, white, smock-like blouse which ended just below her waist.

"What kept you?" she said.

"Florists," he answered.

"You bought me flowers?"

"No. A lady we talked to said her husband bought her a dozen red roses. We checked about ten florists in the immediate and surrounding neighborhoods. Result? No red roses on Valentine's Day. Not to Mrs. Karl Androvich, anyway."

"So?"

"So Steve Carella is uncanny. Can I take off my shoes?"

"Go ahead. I bought two steaks. Do you feel like steaks?"

"Later."

"How is Carella uncanny?"

"Well, he lit into this skinny, pathetic dame as if he were going to rip all the flesh from her bones. When we got outside, I told him I thought he was a little rough with her. I mean, I've seen him operate before, and he usually wears kid gloves with the ladies. So with this one, he used a sledge hammer, and I wondered why. And I told him I disapproved."

"So what did he say?"

"He said he knew she was lying from the minute she opened her mouth, and he began wondering why."

"How did he know?"

"He just knew. That's what was so uncanny about it. We checked all those damn florists, and nobody made a delivery at six in the morning, and none of them were even *open* before nine."

"The husband could have ordered the flowers anywhere in the city, Bert."

"Sure, but that's pretty unlikely, isn't it? He's not a guy who works in an office some place. He's a seaman, and when he's not at sea, he's home. So the logical place to order flowers would be a neighborhood florist."

"So?"

"So nothing. I'm tired. Steve sent a meat cleaver to the lab." He paused. "She didn't look like the kind of a dame who'd use a meat cleaver on a man. Come here."

She went to him, climbing into his lap. He kissed her and said, "I've got the whole weekend. Steve's giving me his Sunday."

"Oh? Yes?"

"You feel funny," he said.

"Funny? How?"

"I don't know. Softer."

"I'm not wearing a bra."

"How come?"

"I wanted to feel free. Keep your hands off me!" she said suddenly, and she leaped out of his lap.

"Now you are the kind of a dame who would use a meat cleaver on a man," Kling said, appraising her from the chair in which he sat.

"Am I?" she answered coolly. "When do you want to eat?"

"Later."

"Where are we going tonight?" Claire asked.

"No place."

"Oh?"

"I don't have to be back at the squad until Monday morning," Kling said.

"Oh, is that right?"

"Yes, and what I planned was . . ."

"Yes?"

"I thought we could get into bed right now and stay

in bed all weekend. Until Monday morning. How does that sound to you?"

"It sounds pretty strenuous."

"Yes, it does. But I vote for it."

"I'll have to think about it. I had my heart set on a movie."

"We can always see a movie," Kling said.

"Anyway, I'm hungry right now," Claire said, studying him narrowly. "I'm going to make the steaks."

"I'd rather go to bed."

"Bert," she said, "man does not live by bed alone." Kling rose suddenly. They stood at opposite ends of the room, studying each other. "What did *you* plan on doing tonight?" he asked.

"Eating steaks," she said.

"And what else?"

"A movie."

"And tomorrow?"

Claire shrugged.

"Come here," he said.

"Come get me," she answered.

He went across the room to her. She tilted her head to his and then crossed her arms tightly over her breasts.

"All weekend," he said.

"You're a braggart," she whispered.

"You're a doll."

"Am I?"

"You're a lovely doll."

"You going to kiss me?"

"Maybe."

They stood not two inches from each other, not touching, staring at each other, savoring this moment, allowing desire to leap between them in a mounting wave.

He put his hands on her waist, but he did not kiss her. Slowly, she uncrossed her arms.

"You really have no bra on?" he asked.

"Big weekend lover," she murmured. "Can't even find out for himself whether or not I have a . . ."

His hands slid under the smock and he pulled Claire to him.

The next time anyone would see Bert Kling would be on Monday morning.

It would still be raining.

Sam Grossman studied the airlines bag for a long time, and then took off his eyeglasses. Grossman was a police lieutenant, a laboratory technician, and the man in charge of the police lab downtown on High Street. In his years of service with the lab, he had seen bodies or portions of bodies in trunks, valises, duffel bags, shopping bags, boxes, and even wrapped in old newspapers. He had never come across one in an airline's overnight bag, but he experienced no sensation of surprise or shock. The inside of the bag was covered with dried blood, but he did not reel back at the sight of it. He knew there was work to be done, and he set about doing it. He was somewhat like a New England farmer discovering that one of his fields would make an excellent pasture if only it were cleared of rocks and stumps. The only way to clear the field was to clear it.

He had already examined the severed hand, and reached the conclusion that it was impossible to get any fingerprint impressions from the badly mutilated fingertips. He had then taken a sampling of blood from the hand for an isoreaction test, and concluded that the blood was in the "O" group.

Now he examined the bag for latent fingerprints, and found none. He had not, in all truth, expected to find any. The person who'd mutilated that hand was a person who was very conscious of fingerprints, a person who would have shown the same caution in handling the bag.

He checked the bag next for microscopic traces of hair or fibers or dust which might give some clue to either the killer's or the victim's identity, occupation, or hobby. He found nothing of value on the outside surface of the bag.

He slit the bag open with a scalpel and studied its inner surface and bottom with a magnifying glass. In one corner of the bag he found what appeared to be remnants of orange chalk dust. He collected several grains for a specimen, put them aside, and then studied the blood stains on the bottom of the bag.

The average layman might have considered Grossman's examination absurd. He was, after all, examining a stain which had obviously been left in the bag by the severed hand. What in the hell was he trying to ascertain? That the hand had been in the bag? Everyone knew that already.

But Grossman was simply trying to determine whether or not the stain on the bottom of the bag was actually human blood; and if not blood, then what? There was the possibility, too, that an apparent bloodstain could have mingled with, or covered, another stain on the bag. And so Grossman really wasn't wasting his time. He was simply doing a thorough job.

The stain was a dark reddish brown in color and, because of the nonabsorbent surface of the bag's bottom, it was somewhat cracked and chipped, resembling a dried mud flat. Grossman gingerly cut out a portion of the stain, and cut this into two smaller portions which he labeled Stain One and Stain Two, for want of a more imaginative nomenclature. He dropped his two specimens into an 0.9 per-cent solution of physiologic salt, and then placed them on separate slides. The slides had to stand in a covered dish for several hours, so he left them and began performing his microscopic and spectroscopic tests on the orange chalk he had found in a corner of the bag. When he returned to the slides later that day, he covered one of them with a coverslip and studied it under a high-power microscope. What he saw was a number of non-nucleated discs, and he knew instantly that the suspect blood was mammalian in origin.

He then took the second slide and poured Wright's Stain onto the unfixed smear, letting it stand for one minute while he timed the operation. Drop by drop, he added distilled water to the slide, waiting for a metallic scum to form on its surface. When the scum had formed, he again consulted his watch, waiting three minutes before he washed and dried the slide.

Using a micrometer eyepiece, he then measured the various cells on the slide. The human red blood corpuscle is about 1/3200 of an inch in diameter. The cell diameter will vary in other animals of the mammalian group, the erythrocyte of the dog—at 1/3500 of an inch—being closest to the human's.

The specimen Grossman examined under his microscope measured 1/3200 of an inch in diameter.

But where measurement dealt with error in thousandths of an inch, Grossman did not want to take any chances. And so he followed the usual laboratory procedure of using a precipitin reaction after either a chemical, microscopic, or spectroscopic test. The precipitin reaction would determine with certainty whether or not the stain was indeed human blood.

The precipitin reaction is a simple one. If you take a rabbit, and if you inject into this rabbit's blood a specimen of whole human blood or human blood serum, something is going to happen. The something that will happen is this: an antibody called a "precipitin" will develop in the rabbit's own serum. This will then react with the proteins of the injected serum. If the reaction is a positive one, the proteins can then be identified as having come from a human being.

The specific reaction to Grossman's stain was positive.

The blood was human.

When he performed his isoreaction test, he learned that it was in the "O" blood group, and he therefore made the logical assumption that the stain on the bottom of the bag had been left by blood dripping from the severed hand and by nothing else.

As for the bits of orange chalk dust, they turned out to be something quite other than chalk. The particles were identified as a woman's cosmetic, further identified through a chemical breakdown and a comparison with the cards in the files as a preparation called Skinglow. Skinglow was a liquid powder base designed to retain face powder in a clinging veil, further designed to add a slight pink glow to very fair skin under makeup.

It was hardly likely that a man would have used it.

And yet the hand in the bag had definitely belonged to a man.

Grossman sighed and passed the information on to the boys of the 87th.

Seven

SATURDAY.

Rain.

Once, when he was a boy, he and some friends had crawled under the iceman's cart on Colby Avenue. It had been pouring bullets, and the three of them sat under the wooden cart and watched the spikes of rain pounding the cobblestones, feeling secure and impervious. Steve Carella caught pneumonia, and shortly afterward the family moved from Isola to Riverhead. He'd always felt the move had been prompted by the fact that he'd caught pneumonia under the iceman's cart on Colby Avenue.

It rained in Riverhead, too. Once he necked with a girl named Grace McCarthy in the basement of her house while the record player oozed "Perfidia," and "Santa Fe Trail," and "Green Eyes," and the rain stained the small crescent-shaped basement window. They were both fifteen, and they had started by dancing, and he had kissed her suddenly and recklessly in the middle of a dip, and then they had curled up on the sofa and listened to Glenn Miller and necked like crazy fools, expecting Grace's mother to come down to the basement at any moment.

Rain wasn't so bad, he supposed.

Sloshing through the puddles with Meyer Meyer on the way to question the second possibility Kling had pulled from the M.P.B. files, Carella cupped his hand around a match, lighted a cigarette, and flipped the match into the water streaming alongside the curb.

"You know that cigarette commercial?" Meyer asked.

60

"Which one?"

"Where the guy is a Thinking Man. You know, a nuclear physist really, but when we first see him he's developing snapshots in a darkroom? You know the one?"

"Yeah, what about it?"

"I got a good one for their series."

"Yeah, let's hear it," Carella said.

"We see this guy working on a safe, you know? He's drilling a hole in the face of the safe, and he's got his safe-cracking tools on the floor, and a couple of sticks of dynamite, like that."

"Yeah, go ahead."

"And the announcer's voice comes in and says, 'Hello there, sir.' The guy looks up from his work and lights a cigarette. The announcer says, 'It must take years of training to become an expert safe-cracker.' The guy smiles politely. 'Oh, I'm not a safe-cracker,' he says. 'Safe-cracking is just a hobby with me. I feel a man should have diversified interests.' The announcer is very surprised. 'Not a safe-cracker?' he asks. 'Just a hobby? May I ask then, sir, what you actually do for a living?'"

"And what does the man at the safe answer?" Carella said.

"The man at the safe blows out a stream of smoke," Meyer said, "and again he smiles politely. 'Certainly, you may ask,' he says. 'I'm a pimp.'" Meyer grinned broadly. "You like it, Steve?"

"Very good. Here's the address. Don't tell jokes to this lady or she may not let us in."

"Who's telling jokes? I may quit this lousy job one day and get a job with an advertising agency."

"Don't do it, Meyer. We couldn't get along without you."

Together, they entered the tenement. The woman they were looking for was named Martha Livingston, and she had reported the absence of her son, Richard, only a week ago. The boy was nineteen years old, six feet two inches tall, and weighed a hundred and ninety-four pounds. These facts, and these alone, qualified him as a candidate for the person who had once owned the severed hand.

"Which apartment is it?" Meyer asked.

"Twenty-four. Second floor front."

They climbed to the second floor. A cat in the hallway mewed and then eyed them suspiciously.

"She smells the law on us," Meyer said. "She thinks we're from the A.S.P.C.A."

"She doesn't know we're really street cleaners," Carella said.

Meyer stooped down to pet the cat as Carella knocked on the door. "Come on, kitty," he said. "Come on, little kitty."

"Who is it?" a woman's voice shouted. The voice sounded startled.

"Mrs. Livingston?" Carella said to the door.

"Yes? Who is it?"

"Police," Carella said. "Would you open the door, please?"

"Po—"

And then there was silence.

The silence was a familiar one. It was the silence of sudden discovery and hurried pantomime. Whatever was going on behind that tenement door, Mrs. Livingston was not in the apartment alone. The silence persisted. Meyer's hand left the cat's head and went up to the holster clipped to the right side of his belt. He looked at Carella curiously. Carella's .38 was already in his hand.

"Mrs. Livingston?" Carella called.

There was no answer from within the apartment.

"Mrs. Livingston?" he called again, and Meyer braced himself against the opposite wall, waiting. "Okay, kick it in," Carella said.

Meyer brought back his right leg, shoved himself off the wall with his left shoulder, and smashed his foot against the lock in a flat-footed kick that sent the door splintering inward. He rushed into the room behind the opening door, gun in hand.

"Hold it!" he yelled, and a thin man in the process of stepping out onto the fire escape, one leg over the sill, the other still in the room, hesitated for a moment, undecided.

"You'll get wet out there, mister," Meyer said.

The man hesitated a moment longer, and then came back into the room. Meyer glanced at his feet. He was wearing no socks. He glanced sheepishly at the woman who stood opposite him near the bed. The woman was wearing a slip. There was nothing under it. She was a big blowzy dame of about forty-five with hennaed hair and a drunkard's faded eyes.

"Mrs. Livingston?" Carella asked.

"Yeah," she said. "What the hell do you mean busting in here?"

"What was your friend's hurry?" Carella asked.

"I'm in no hurry," the thin man answered.

"No? You always leave a room by the window?"

"I wanted to see if it was still raining."

"It's still raining. Get over here."

"What did I do?" the man asked, but he moved quickly to where the two detectives were standing. Methodically, Meyer frisked him, his hands pausing when he reached the man's belt. He pulled a revolver from the man's waist and handed it to Carella.

"You got a permit for this?" Carella asked.

"Yeah," the man said.

"You'd better have. What's your name, mister?"

"Cronin," he said. "Leonard Cronin."

"Why were you in such a hurry to get out of here, Mr. Cronin?"

"You don't have to answer nothing, Lennie," Mrs. Livingston said.

"You a lawyer, Mrs. Livingston?" Meyer said.

"No, but . . ."

"Then stop giving advice. We asked you a question, Mr. Cronin."

"Don't tell him nothing, Lennie."

"Look, Lennie," Meyer said patiently, "we got all the time in the world, either here or up at the squad, so you just decide what you're going to say, and then say it. In the meantime, go put on your socks, and you better put on a robe or something, Mrs. Livingston, before we get the idea a little hanky-panky was going on in this room. Okay?"

"I don't need no robe," Mrs. Livingston said. "What I got, you seen before."

"Yeah, but put on the robe anyway. We wouldn't want you to catch cold."

"Don't worry about me catching cold, you son-of-a-bitch," Mrs. Livingston said.

"Nice talk," Meyer answered, shaking his head. Cronin, sitting on the edge of the bed, was pulling on his socks. He was wearing black trousers. A black raincoat was draped over a wooden chair in the corner of the room. A black umbrella dripped water onto the floor near the night-table.

"You were forgetting your raincoat and umbrella, weren't you, Lennie?" Carella said.

Cronin looked up from lacing his shoes. "I guess so."

"You'd both better come along with us," Carella said. "Put on some clothes, Mrs. Livingston."

Mrs. Livingston seized her left breast with her left hand. She aimed it like a pistol at Carella, squeezed it briefly and angrily, and shouted, "In your eye, cop!"

"Okay, then, come along the way you are. We can add indecent exposure to the prostitution charge the minute we hit the street."

"Prosti—! What the hell are you talking about? Boy, you got a nerve!"

"Yeah, I know," Carella said. "Let's go, let's go."

"Why'd you have to bust in here anyway?" Mrs. Livingston said. "What do you want?"

"We come to ask you some questions about your missing son, that's all," Carella said.

"My son? Is that what this is all about? I hope the bastard is dead. Is that why you broke down the door, for Christ's sake?"

"If you hope he's dead, why'd you bother to report him missing?"

"So I could get relief checks. He was my sole means of support. The minute he took off, I applied for relief.

And I had to report him missing to make it legit. That's why. You think I care whether he's dead or alive? Some chance!"

"You're a nice lady, Mrs. Livingston," Meyer said.

"I am a nice lady," she answered. "Is there something wrong about a matinee with the man you love?"

"Not if your husband doesn't disapprove."

"My husband is dead," she said. "And in hell."

"You both behave as if there was a little more than that going on, Mrs. Livingston," Carella said. "Get dressed. Meyer, take a look through the apartment."

"You got a search warrant?" the little man asked. "You got no right to go through this place without a warrant."

"You're absolutely right, Lennie," Carella said. "We'll come back with one."

"I know my rights," Cronin said.

"Sure."

"I know my rights."

"How about it, lady? Dressed or naked, you're coming over to the station house. Now which will it be?"

"In your eye!" Lady Livingston said.

The patrolmen downstairs all managed to drop up to the Interrogation Room on one pretense or another to take a look at the fat redheaded slob who sat answering questions in her slip. Andy Parker said to Miscolo in the Clerical Office, "we take a mug shot of her like that, and we'll be able to peddle the photos for five bucks apiece."

"This precinct got glamour, that's what it's got," Miscolo answered, and he went back to his typing.

Parker and Hawes went downtown for the search warrant. Upstairs, Meyer and Carella and Lieutenant Byrnes interrograted the two suspects. Byrnes, because he was an older man and presumably less susceptible to the mammalian display, interrogated Martha Livingston in the Interrogation Room off the corridor. Meyer and Carella talked to Leonard Cronin in a corner of the squadroom, far from Lennie's overexposed paramour.

"Now, how about it, Lennie?" Meyer said. "You really got a permit for this rod, or are you just snowing us? Come on, you can talk to us."

"Yeah, I got a permit," Cronin said. "Would I kid you guys?"

"I don't think you'd try to kid us, Lennie," Meyer said gently, "and we won't try to kid you, either. I can't tell you very much about this, but it can be very serious, take my word for it."

"How do you mean serious?"

"Well, let's say there could be a lot more involved here than just a Sullivan Act violation. Let's put it that way."

"You mean because I was banging Martha when you come in? Is that what you mean?"

"No, not that, either. Let's say there is a very big juicy crime involved here maybe. And let's say you could find yourself right in the middle of it. Okay? So level with us from the start, and things may go easier for you."

"I don't know what big juicy crime you're talking about," Cronin said.

"Well, you think about it a little," Carella said.

"You mean the gat? Okay, I ain't got a permit. Is that what you mean?"

"Well, that's not too serious, Lennie," Meyer said. "No, we're not thinking about the pistol."

"Then what? You mean like because Martha's husband ain't really croaked? You mean like because you got us on adultery?"

"Well, even that isn't too serious, Lennie," Carella said. "*That* we can talk about.

"Then what? The junk?"

"The *junk*, Lennie?"

"Yeah, in the room."

"Heroin, Lennie?"

"No, no, hey, no, nothing big like that. The mootah. Just a few sticks, though. Just for kicks. That ain't so serious, now is it?"

"No, that could be very minor, Lennie. Depending on how much marijuana you had there in the room."

"Oh, just a few sticks."

"Well then, you've only got a possession rap to worry about. You weren't planning on selling any of that stuff, were you, Lennie?"

"No, no, hey, no, it was just for kicks, just for me and Martha, like you know for kicks. We lit a few sticks before we hopped between the sheets."

"Then that's not too serious, Lennie."

"So what's so serious?"

"The boy."

"What boy?"

"Martha's son. Richard, that's his name, isn't it?"

"How do I know? I never even met the kid."

"You never met him? How long have you known Martha?"

"I met her last night. In a bar. A joint called The Short-Snorter, you know it? It's run by these two guys, they used to be in the China-Burma-India . . ."

"You only met her last night?"

"Sure."

"She said you were the man she loved," Carella said.

"Yeah, it was love at first sight."

"And you never met her son?"

"Never."

"You ever fly, Lennie?"

"Fly? How do you mean fly? You talking about the marijuana again?"

"No, fly. In an airplane."

"Never. Just catch me dead in one of them things!"

"How long have you gone for black, Lennie?"

"Black? How do you mean black?"

"Your clothes. Your pants, your tie, your raincoat, your umbrella. Black."

"I bought them for a funeral," Cronin said.

"Whose funeral?"

"A buddy of mine. We used to run a crap game together."

"You ran a crap game, too, Lennie? You've been a busy little man, haven't you?"

"Oh, this wasn't nothing illegal. We never played for money."

"And your friend died recently, is that right?"

"Yeah. The other day. So I bought the black clothes. Out of respect. You can check. I can tell you the place where I bought them."

"We'd appreciate that, Lennie. But you didn't own these clothes on Wednesday, did you?"

"Wednesday. Now let me think a minute. What's today?"

"Today is Saturday."

"Yeah, that's right, Saturday. No. I bought the clothes Thursday. You can check it. They probably got a record."

"How about you, Lennie?"

"How about me? How do you mean how about me?"

"Have *you* got a record?"

"Well, a little one."

"How little?"

"I done a little time once. A stickup. Nothing serious."

"You may do a little more," Carella said. "But nothing serious."

In the Interrogation Room, Lieutenant Byrnes said, "You're a pretty forthright woman, Mrs. Livingston, aren't you?"

"I don't like being dragged out of my house in the middle of the morning," Martha said.

"Weren't you embarrassed about going downstairs in your slip?"

"No. I keep my body good. I got a good body."

"What were you and Mr. Cronin trying to hide, Mrs. Livingston?"

"Nothing. We're in love. I'll shout it from the rooftops."

"Why did he try to get out of that room?"

"He wasn't trying to get out. He told them what he was trying to do. He wanted to see if it was still raining."

"So he was climbing out on the fire escape to do that, right?"

"Yeah."

"Are you aware that your son Richard could be dead at this moment, Mrs. Livingston?"

"Who cares? Good riddance to bad rubbish. The people he was hanging around with, he's better off dead. I raised a bum instead of a son."

"What kind of people was he hanging around with?"

"A gang, a street gang, it's the same story every place in this lousy city. You try to raise a kid right, and what happens? Please, don't get me started."

"Did your son tell you he was leaving home?"

"No. I already gave all this to another detective when I reported him missing. I don't know where he is, and I don't give a damn, as long as I get my relief checks. Now that's that."

"You told the arresting officers your husband was dead. Is that true?"

"He's dead."

"When did he die?"

"Three years ago."

"Did he die, or did he leave?"

"It's the same thing, isn't it?"

"Not exactly."

"He left."

The room was suddenly very silent.

"Three years ago?"

"Three years ago. When Dickie was just sixteen. He packed up and left. It ain't so easy to raise a boy alone. It ain't so easy. And now he's gone, too. Men stink. They all stink. They all want one thing. Okay, I'll give it to them. But not here." She tapped her chest. "Not here inside, where it counts. They all stink. Every single one of them."

"Do you think your son might have run off with some of his friends?"

"I don't know what he done, the little bastard, and I don't care. Gratitude. I raised him alone after his father left. And this is what I get. He runs out on me. Quits his job and runs out. He's just like all the rest of them, they all stink. You can't trust any man alive. I hope he drops dead, wherever he is. I hope the little bastard drops . . ."

And suddenly she was weeping.

She sat quite still in the chair, a woman of forty-five with ridiculously flaming red hair, a big-breasted woman who sat attired only in a silk slip, a fat woman with the faded eyes of a drunkard, and her shoulders did not move, and her face did not move, and her hands did not move, she sat quite still in the hard-backed wooden chair while the tears ran down her face and her nose got red and her teeth clamped into her lips.

"Running out on me," she said, and then she didn't say anything else. She sat stiffly in the chair, fighting the tears that coursed down her cheeks and her neck and stained the front of her slip.

"I'll get you a coat or something, Mrs. Livingston," Byrnes said.

"I don't need a coat. I don't care who sees me. I don't care. Everybody can see what I am. One look, and everybody can see what I am. I don't need a coat. A coat ain't going to hide nothing."

Byrnes left her alone in the room, weeping stiffly in the hard-backed chair.

They found exactly thirty-four ounces of marijuana in Martha Livingston's apartment. Apparently, Leonard Cronin was not a very good mathematician. Apparently, too, he was in slightly more serious trouble than he had originally presumed. If, as he'd stated, there had only been a stick or two of marijuana in the room—enough to have made at least two ounces of the stuff—he'd have been charged with possession, which particular crime was punishable by imprisonment of from two to ten years. Now *thirty-four* ounces ain't *two* ounces. And possession of sixteen ounces or more of narcotics other than heroin, morphine, or cocaine created a *rebuttable* presumption of intent to sell, the "rebuttable" meaning that Cronin could claim he hadn't intended selling it at all, at all. And the maximum term of imprisonment for possession with intent to sell was ten years, the difference between the two charges being that a simple possession rap would usually draw a lesser prison term whereas an intent to sell rap usually drew the limit.

But Cronin had a few other things to worry about. By his own admission, he and Martha Livingston had lit a few sticks before hopping into bed together and Section 2010 of the Penal Law quite bluntly stated: "Perpetration of an act of intercourse with a female not one's wife who is under the influence of narcotics is punishable by an indeterminate sentence of one day to life or a maximum of twenty years."

When the gun charge was added to this, and the running of an illegal crap game considered, even if one wished to forget the simple charge of simple adultery—a misdemeanor punishable by imprisonment in a penitentiary or county jail for not more than six months, or by a fine of not more than two hundred and fifty bucks, or by both—even if one wished to forget this minor infraction, Leonard Cronin was going to be a busier little man than he had ever been.

As for Martha Livingston, she'd have been better off exploring Africa. Even allowing for her own conviction that all men stank, she had certainly chosen a prize this time. The narcotics, whomever they belonged to, had been found in her pad. The lady who'd fallen in love at first sight was going to have a hell of a tough row to hoe.

But whatever else lay ahead for the hapless lovers, homicide and butchery would not be included in the charges against them. A check with the clothing store Leonard Cronin named proved that he had indeed purchased his funeral outfit on Thursday. A further check of his rooming-house closet showed that he owned no other black garments. And neither did Mrs. Livingston.

There must be a God, after all.

Eight

ON SUNDAY MORNING, Cotton Hawes went to church in the rain before reporting to work.

When he came out, it was still raining and he felt much the same as he'd felt before the services. He didn't know why he expected to feel any different; he'd certainly never been washed by any of the great religious fervor which had possessed his minister father. But every Sunday, rain or shine, Cotton Hawes went to church. And every Sunday he sat and listened to the sermon, and he recited the psalms, and he waited. He didn't know exactly what he was waiting for. He suspected he was waiting for a bolt of lightning and an ear-splitting crash of thunder which would suddenly reveal the face of God. He supposed that all he really wanted to see was a glimpse of something which was not quite so *real* as the things that surrounded him every day of the week.

For whatever else could be said about police work—and there were countless things to be said, and countless things being said—no one could deny that it presented its practitioners with a view of life which was as real as bread crumbs. Police work dealt with essentials, raw instincts and basic motives, stripped of all the hoop-dee-dah of the sterilized, compressed-in-a-vacuum civilization of the twentieth century. As he walked through the rain, Hawes thought it odd that most of the time consumed by people was spent in sharing the fantasies of another. A thousand escape hatches from reality were available to every manjack in the world—books, the motion pictures, television, magazines, plays, concerts, ballets, anything or everything designed to substitute a pretense of reality, a semblance of real life, a fantasy world for a flesh-and-blood one.

Now perhaps it was wrong for a cop to be thinking this way, Hawes realized, because a cop was one of the fantasy figures in one of the world's escapes: the mystery novel. The trouble was, he thought, that only the fantasy cop was the hero while the *real* cop was just a person. It seemed somehow stupid to him that the most honored people in the world were those who presented the fantasies, the actors, the directors, the writers, all the various performers whose sole reason for being was to entertain. It was as if a very small portion of the world was actually alive, and these people were alive only in so far as they performed in created fantasies. The rest of the people were observing; the rest of the people were spectators. It would not have been half so sad if these people were viewing the spectacle of real life. Instead, they were observing only a representation of life, so that they became twice-removed from life itself.

Even conversation seemed to concern itself primarily with the fantasy world, and not the real. Did you see Jack Paar last night? Have you read *Doctor Zhivago?* Wasn't *Dragnet* exciting? Did you see the review of *Sweet Bird of Youth?* Talk, talk, talk, but all of the talk had as its nucleus the world of make-believe. And now the television programs had carried this a step further. More and more channels were featuring people who simply talked about things, so that even the burden of talking about the make-believe world had been removed from the observer's shoulders—there were now other people who would talk it over *for* him. Life became thrice-removed.

And in the midst of this thrice-removed existence, there was reality, and reality for a cop was a hand severed at the wrist.

Now what the hell would they do with that hand on *Naked City?*

He didn't know. He only knew that every Sunday he went to church and looked for something.

On this Sunday, he came out feeling the same as when he'd gone in, and he walked along the shining wet sidewalk bordering the park, heading for the station house. The green globes had been turned on in defense against the rain, the numerals "87" glowing feebly against the slanting gray. He looked up at the dripping stone façade, climbed the low flat steps and entered the muster room. Dave Murchison was sitting behind the desk, reading a movie magazine. The cover showed a picture of Debbie Reynolds, and the headline asked the provocative question *What Will Debbie Do Now?*

He followed the pointing arrow of the DETECTIVE DIVISION sign, climbed the metal steps to the second story, and walked down the long, dim corridor. He shoved through the gate in the slatted railing, tossed his hat at the rack in the corner, and went to his desk. The squadroom was oddly silent. He felt almost as if he were in church again. Frankie Hernandez, a Puerto Rican cop who'd been born and raised in the precinct neighborhood, looked up and said,"Hi, Cotton."

"Hello, Frankie," he said. "Steve come in yet?"

"He called in about ten minutes ago," Hernandez answered. "Said to tell you he was going straight to the docks to talk to the captain of the *Farren*."

"Okay," Hawes said. "Anything else?"

"Got a report from Grossman on the meat cleaver."

"What mea—oh yeah, yeah, the Androvich woman." He paused. "Any luck?"

"Negative. Not a thing on it but yesterday's roast."

"Where is everybody, anyway?" Hawes asked. "It's so quiet around here."

"There was a burglary last night, grocery store on Culver. Andy and Meyer are out on it. The loot called in to say he'd be late. Wife's got a fever, and he's waiting for the doctor."

"Isn't Kling supposed to be in today?"

Hernandez shook his head. "Swapped with Carella."

"Who's catching, anyway?" Hawes said. "You got a copy of the duty sheet around?"

"I'm catching," Hernandez said.

"Boy, it sure is quiet around here," Hawes said. "Is Miscolo around? I'd like some tea."

"He was here a little while ago. I think he went down to talk to the Captain."

"Days like this . . ." Hawes started, and then let the sentence trail. After a while, he said, "Frankie, you ever get the feeling that life just isn't real?"

Perhaps he'd asked the wrong person. Life, to Frankie Hernandez, was very real indeed. Hernandez, you see, had taken upon himself the almost impossible task of proving to the world at large that Puerto Ricans could be the *good* guys in life's little drama. He did not know who'd been handling his people's press relations before he happened upon the scene, but he did know that someone was handling it all wrong. He had never had the urge to mug anyone, or knife anyone, or even to have a single puff of a marijuana cigarette. He had grown up in the territory of the 87th Precinct, in one of the worst slums in the world, and he had never so much as stolen a postage stamp, or even a sidelong glance at the whores who paraded *La Via de Putas.* He was a devout Catholic whose father worked hard for a living, and whose mother was concerned solely with the proper upbringing of the four children she had brought into the world. When Hernandez decided to become a cop, his mother and father approved heartily. He became a rookie when he was twenty-two years old, after having served a four-year hitch in the Marines and distinguishing himself in combat during the hell that was Iwo Jima. In his father's candy store, a picture of Frankie Hernandez in full battle dress was pasted to the mirror behind the counter, alongside the Coca Cola sign. Frankie's father never failed to tell any stranger in the store that the picture was of his son Frankie who was now "a detective in the city's police."

It hadn't been easy for Hernandez to become a detective in the city's police. To begin with, he'd found a certain amount of prejudice within the department itself, brotherhood edicts notwithstanding. And, coupled with this was a rather peculiar attitude on the part of some of the citizens of the precinct. They felt, he soon discovered, that since he was "one of them" he was expected to look the other way whenever they became involved in police trouble. Well, unfortunately, Frankie Hernandez was incapable of looking the other way. He had sworn the oath, and he was now wearing the uniform, and he had a job to perform.

And besides, there was The Cause.

Frankie Hernandez had to prove to the neighborhood, the people of the neighborhood, the police department, the city, and maybe even the world that Puerto Ricans were people. Colleagues the likes of Andy Parker sometimes made The Cause difficult. Before Andy Parker, there had been patrolmen colleagues who'd made The Cause just as difficult. Hernandez imagined that if he ever became Chief of Detectives or even Police Commissioner, there would be Andy Parkers surrounding those high offices, too, ever ready to remind him that The Cause was something to be fought constantly, day and night.

So for Frankie Hernandez, life was always real. Sometimes, in fact, it got too goddamn real.

"No, I never got that feeling, Cotton," he said.

"I guess it's the rain," Hawes answered, and he yawned.

The S. S. Farren had been named after a famous and honorable White Plains gentleman called Jack Farren. But whereas the flesh-and-blood Farren was a kind, amiable, sympathetic, lovable coot who always carried a clean handkerchief, the namesake looked like a ship which was mean, rotten, rusty, dirty and snot-nosed.

The captain of the ship looked the same way.

He was a hulk of a man with a three-days' beard stubble on his chin. He picked his teeth with a matchbook cover all the while Carella talked to him, sucking air interminably in an attempt to loosen breakfast from his molars. They sat in the captain's cabin, a coffin of a compartment, the bulkheads of which dripped sweat and rust. The captain sucked at his teeth and prodded with his soggy matchbook cover. The rain slanted outside the single porthole. The compartment stank of living, of food, of human waste.

"What can you tell me about Karl Androvich?" Carella asked.

"What do you want to know?" the captain said. His name was Kissovsky. He sounded like a bear. He moved with all the subtle grace of a Panzer division.

"Has he been sailing with you long?"

Kissovsky shrugged. "Two, three years. He in trouble? What did he get himself into since he jumped ship?"

"Nothing that we know of. Is he a good sailor?"

"Good as most. Sailors ain't worth a damn today. When I was a young man, sailors was sailors." He sucked air between his teeth.

"Ships were made of wood," Carella said, "and men were made of iron."

"What? Oh, yeah." Kissovsky tried a smile which somehow formed as a leer. "I ain't that old, buddy," he said. "But we had siilors when I was a kid, not beatniks looking for banana boats so they can practice that . . . what do you call it . . . Zen? And then come back to write about it. We had men! Men!"

"Then Androvich wasn't a good sailor?"

"Good as most until he jumped ship," Kissovsky said. "The minute he jumped ship, he became a bad sailor. I had to make the run down with a man short in the crew. I had the crew stretched tight as it was. One man short didn't help the situation any, I can tell you. A ship is like a little city, buddy. There's guys that sweep the streets, and guys that run the trains, and guys that turn on the lights at night, and guys that run the restaurants, and that's what makes the city go, you see. Okay. You lose the guy who turns on the lights, so nobody can see. You lose the guy who runs the restaurant, so nobody eats. Either that, or you got to find somebody else to do the job, and that means taking him away from another job, so no matter how you slice it, it screws up the china closet. Androvich screwed up the china closet real fine. Besides, he was a lousy sailor, anyway."

"How so?"

"Out for kicks," Kissovsky said, tossing one hand upward in a salute to God. "Live, live, burn, burn, bright like a Roman candle, bullshit! Every port we hit, Androvich went ashore and come back drunk as a fish. And dames? All over the lot! It's a wonder this guy didn't come down with the Oriental Crud or something, the way he was knocking around. Kicks! That's all he was looking for. Kicks!"

"A girl in every port, huh?" Carella said.

"Sure, and drunk as a pig. I used to tell him you got a sweet little wife waiting for you home, you want to bring her back a present from one of these exotic tomatoes, is that what you want to do? He used to laugh at me. Ha, ha, ha. Big joke. Life was a big joke. So he jumps ship, and he screws up the chocolate pudding. That's a sailor, huh?"

"Did he have a girl in this city, too, Captain Kissovsky?"

"Lay off the captain crap, huh?" Kissovsky said. "Call me Artie, okay, and I'll call you George or whatever the hell your name is, and that way we cut through the fog, okay?"

"It's Steve."

"Okay. Steve. That's a good name. I got a brother named Steve. He's strong as an ox. He can lift a Mack truck with his bare hands, that kid."

"Artie, did Androvich have a girl in this city?"

Kissovsky sucked air through his teeth, maneuvered the matchbook folder around the back of his mouth, and thought. He spit a sliver of food onto the deck, shrugged, and said, "I don't know."

"Who *would* know?"

"Maybe the other guys in the crew, but I doubt it. Anything happens on this tub, I know about it. I can tell you one thing. He didn't spend his nights sitting around holding hands with little Lulu Belle or whatever the hell her name is."

"Meg? His wife?"

"Yeah, Meg. The one he's got tattooed on his arm there. The one he picked up in Atlanta. Beats me how she ever got him to come up with a ring." Kissovsky shrugged. "Anyway, she did get him to marry her, but that don't mean she also got him to sit home tatting doilies. No, sir. This kid was out to live! No doilies for him. Doilies are for the Sands Spit commuters, not for the Karl Androviches. You know what he'd do?"

"What?" Carella asked.

"We'd pull into port, you know. I mean here, this city. So he'd wait like two weeks, living it up all over town, shooting his roll, before he'd call home to say we were in. And maybe this was like about two days before we were going to pull out again. Buddy, this kid was giving that girl the business in both ears. She seems like a nice kid, too. I feel a little sorry for her." He shrugged and spit onto the deck again.

"Where'd he go?" Carella asked. "When he wasn't home? Where'd he hang out?"

"Wherever there are dames," Kissovsky said.

"There are dames all over the city."

"Then that's where he hung out. All over the city. I'll bet you a five-dollar bill he's with some dame right now. He'll drop in on little Scarlett O'Hara or whatever the hell her name is, the minute he runs out of money."

"He only had thirty dollars with him when he vanished," Carella said.

"Thirty dollars, my eye! Who told you that? There was a big crap game on the way up from Pensacola. Androvich was one of the winners. Took away something like seven hundred bucks. That ain't hay, Steve-oh. Add to that all of January's pay, you know we were holding it until we hit port, and that adds up to quite a little bundle. And we were only in port here two days. We docked on the twelfth, and we were shoving off on the fourteenth, Valentine's Day. So a guy can't spend more than a grand in two days, can he?" Kissovsky paused thoughtfully. "The way I figure it, he started back for the ship, picked up some floozie, and has been living it high on the hog with her for the past month or so. When the loot runs out, Androvich'll be home."

"You think he's just having himself a fling, is that it?"

"Just running true to form, that's all. In Nagasaki, when we was there, this guy . . . well, that's another story." He paused. "You ain't worried about him, are you?"

"Well . . ."

"Don't be. Check the whore houses, and the strip joints, and the bars, and Skid Row. You'll find him, all right. Only thing is, I don't think he *wants* to be found. So what're you gonna do when you latch onto him? *Force* him to go back to Melissa Lee, or whatever the hell her name is?"

"No, we couldn't do that," Carella said.

"So what the hell are you bothering for?" Kissovsky sucked air through his teeth and then spat on the deck. "Stop worrying," he said. "He'll turn up."

The garbage cans were stacked in the areaway between the two tenements, and the rain had formed small pools of water on the lid of each can. The old woman was wearing house slippers, and so she stepped gingerly into the areaway and tried to avoid the water underfoot, walking carefully to the closest garbage can, carrying her bag of garbage clutched to her breast like a sucking infant.

She lifted the lid of the can and shook the water free and was about to drop her bag into the can when she saw that it was filled. The old lady was Irish, and she unleashed a torrent of swear words which would have turned a leprechaun blue, replaced the lid and went to the second garbage can. She was thoroughly drenched now, and she cursed the fact that she hadn't thought to bring an umbrella down with her, cursed the lid of the second garbage can because it seemed to be stuck, finally wrenched it free, soaking herself anew with the water that had been resting on it, and prepared to toss her bag into it and run like hell for the building.

Then she saw the newspaper.

She hesitated for a moment.

The newspaper had been wrapped around something, but the wrapping had come loose. Curiously, the old lady bent closer to the garbage can.

And then she let out a shriek.

Nine

EVERYTHING HAPPENED on Monday.

To begin with, Blaney—the assistant medical examiner—officially studied the delightful little package which the patrolmen had dug out of the garbage can after a frantic call from the old lady.

The bloody newspaper contained a human hand.

And after duly examining this hand, Blaney phoned the 87th to say that it had belonged to a white male between the ages of 18 and 24, and that unless he was greatly mistaken, it was the mate to the hand he had examined the week before.

Bert Kling took the telephoned message. He barely had strength enough to hold the pencil in his hand as he wrote down the information.

That was the first thing that happened on Monday, and it happened at 9:30 in the morning.

The second thing happened at 11:00 A.M. and it seemed as if the second occurrence would solve once and for all the problem of identification. The second occurrence involved a body which had been washed ashore on the banks of the River Harb. The body had no arms and no head. It was promptly shipped off to the morgue where several things were learned about it.

To begin with, the body was clothed and a wallet in the right hip pocket of the trousers carried a sopping-wet identification card and a driver's license. The man in the water was known as George Rice. A call to the number listed on the identification card confirmed Blaney's estimate that the body had been in the river for close to two weeks. Apparently, Mr. Rice had failed to come home from work one night two weeks ago. His wife had reported him missing, and a sheet on him was allegedly in the files of the M.P.B. Mrs. Rice was asked to come down to identify the remains as soon as she was able to. In the meantime, Blaney continued his examination.

And he decided, even though Mr. Rice had been only twenty-six years old, and even though Mr. Rice was lacking arms and a head, and even though Mr. Rice was a good possibility for the person who had owned the two hands that had turned up—he decided after a thorough examination that the body had apparently lost its head and arms through contact with the propeller blades of either a ship or a large boat. And whereas the blood stain on the bottom of the airline bag had belonged to the "O" group, the blood of Mr. Rice checked out as belonging to the "AB" group. And whereas the hugeness of the two hands indicated a big fellow, Mr. Rice, allowing for his missing head, added up to five feet eight and a half inches, and that is not big.

When Mrs. Rice identified the remains through her husband's clothing and a scar on his abdomen—the clothing was not in such excellent shape after having been put through the rigorous test of contact with a boat's propeller and submersion for two weeks, but the scar was still intact—when she made the identification, she also stated that Mr. Rice worked in the next state and that he took a ferry to work each morning and returned by ferry each evening, and it therefore seemed more than likely that Mr. Rice had either jumped, been pushed, or had fallen from the stern of the ferry and thereby been mutilated by the boat's propellers. A thorough search of the Rice apartment that same day uncovered a suicide note.

And so it was Blaney's unfortunate duty to call the 87th once more and report to Kling, the weary weekend horseman, that the hands he'd been examining over the past few days did *not* belong to the body which had been washed ashore that morning.

So that was that, and the problem of identification still remained to be solved, with the young son of Martha Livingston and the young sailor Karl Androvich still shaping up as pretty good possibilities.

But it was still Monday, a very blue Monday at that because it was raining, and everything was going to happen on Monday.

At 2:00 P.M. the third thing happened.

Two hoodlums were picked up in the next state, and both gave the police address in Isola. A teletype to City Headquarters requesting information netted a B-sheet for one of them, but no record for the other. The boys, it seemed, had held up a Shell station and then tried a hasty escape in a beat-up automobile. So hasty was their departure that they neglected to notice a police car which was cruising along the highway, with the result that they smacked right into the front right fender of the approaching black-and-white sedan, and that was the end of *that* little caper. The boy carrying the gun, the one with the record, was named Robert Germaine.

The other boy, the sloppy driver who'd slammed into the motor patrol car, was named Richard Livingston.

No matter how sloppily you drive a car, it takes two hands—and Richard Livingston was in possession of both of his.

Kling got the information at 3:00 P.M. With weary, shaking fingers, he wrote it down and reminded himself to tell Carella to chalk off a possible victim.

At 4:10 P.M. the telephone rang again.

"Hello," Kling said.

"Who's this?" a woman's voice asked.

"This is Detective Kling, 87th Squad. Who's this?"

"Mrs. Androvich," the voice said. "Mrs. Karl Androvich."

"Oh. Hello, Mrs. Androvich. What's wrong?"

"Nothing's wrong," she said.

"I mean, what . . ."

"My husband's back," Meg Androvich said.

"Karl?"

"Yes."

"He's back?"

"Yes."

"When did he return?"

"Just a few minutes ago," she said. She paused for a long time. Then she said, "He brought me flowers."

"I'm glad he's back," Kling said. "I'll notify the Missing Persons Bureau. Thank you for calling."

"Not at all," Meg said. "Would you do me a favor, please?"

"What's that, Mrs. Androvich?"

"Would you please tell that other detective? Carella? Was that his name?"

"Yes, ma'am."

"Would you please tell him?"

"That your husband's back? Yes, ma'am, I'll tell him."

"No, not that. That's not what I want you to tell him."

"What *do* you want me to tell him, Mrs. Androvich?"

"That Karl brought me flowers. Tell him that, would you? That Karl brought me flowers." And she hung up.

So that was what happened on Monday.

And that was everything.

The boys still had a pair of hands to work with, and nobody seemed to belong to those hands.

On Tuesday, there was a street rumble, and a fire in the neighborhood, and a woman who clobbered her husband with a frying pan, and so everybody was pretty busy.

On Wednesday, Steve Carella came back to work. It was still raining. It seemed as if it would never stop raining. A week had gone by since Patrolman Genero had found the first hand.

A whole week had gone by, and the boys were right back where they'd started.

Ten

THE OLD WOMAN who'd discovered the second hand in the garbage can was named Colleen Brady. She was sixty-four years old, but there was about her a youthfulness which complied faithfully to her given name, so that indeed she seemed to be a colleen.

There is an image that comes instantly to mind whenever an Irish girl is mentioned, an image compounded of one part Saint Patrick's Day to three parts John Huston's *The Quiet One*. The girl has red hair and green eyes, and she runs through the heather beneath a sky of shrieking blue billowing with clouds of pure white, and there is a wild smile on her mouth and you know she will slap you silly if you try to touch her. She is Irish and wild and savage and pure and young, forever young, forever youthful.

And so was Colleen Brady.

She entertained Carella and Hawes as if they were beaux come to call on her with sprigs of hollyhock. She served them tea, and she told them jokes in a brogue as thick as good Irish coffee. Her eyes were green and bright and her skin was as smooth and as fair as a seventeen-year-old's. Her hair was white, but you knew with certainty that it had once been red, and her narrow waist could still be spanned by a man with big hands.

"I saw no one," she told the detectives. "Nary a soul. It was a day to keep indoors, it was. I saw one one in the hallway, and no one on the stairs, and no one in the courtyard. It was a right bitter day, and I should have carried down me umbrella, but I didn't. I like to have died from faint when I saw what was in that garbage can. Will y'have more tea?"

"No, thank you, Mrs. Brady. You saw no one?"

"No one, aye. And I'm sorry I can't be of more help, for 'tis a gruesome thing to cut a man apart, a gruesome thing. 'Tis a thing for barbarians." She paused, sipping at her tea, her green eyes alert in her narrow face. "Have you tried the neighbors? Have you asked them? Perhaps they saw."

"We wanted to talk to you first, Mrs. Brady," Hawes said.

She nodded. "Are you Irish, young man?" she asked.

"Part."

Her green eyes glowed. She nodded secretly and said nothing more, but she studied Hawes with the practiced eye of a young girl who'd been chased around the village green more than once.

"Well, we'll be going now, Mrs. Brady," Carella said. "Thank you very much."

"Try the neighbors," she told them. "Maybe they saw. Maybe one of them saw."

None of them had seen.

They tried every apartment in Mrs. Brady's building and the building adjoining it. Then, wearily, they trudged back to the squadroom in the rain. Hernandez had a message for Carella the moment he walked in.

"Steve, got a call about a half-hour ago from a guy at the M.P.B. He asked for Kling, but I told him he was out, and he wanted to know who else was on the case of the hand in the airline bag, so I told him you were. He said either you or Kling should call him back the minute either of you got in."

"What's his name?" Carella asked.

"It's on the pad there. Bartholomew or something."

Carella sat at his desk and pulled the pad over. "Romeo Bartholdi," he said aloud, and he dialed the Missing Persons Bureau.

"Hello," he said, "this is Carella at the 87th Precinct. We got a call here a little while ago from some guy named Bartholdi, said he . . ."

"This is Bartholdi."

"Hi. What's up?"

"What'd you say your name was?"

"Carella."

"Hello, *paisan*."

"Hello," Carella said, smiling. "What's this all about?"

"Look, I know this is none of my business. But something occurred to me."

"What is it?"

"A guy named Kling was in last week some time looking through the files. I got to talking to him later, and he told me how you guys found a hand in an airline overnight bag. A guy's hand."

"Yeah, that's right," Carella said. "What about it?"

"Well, *paisan*, this is none of my business. Only he was looking for a possible connection with a disappearance, and he was working through the February stuff, you know."

"Yeah?"

"He said the bag belonged to an outfit called Circle Airlines, am I right?"

"That's right," Carella said.

"Okay. This may be reaching, but here it is anyway, for whatever it's worth. My partner and I have been trying to track down a dame who vanished about three weeks ago. She's a stripper, came here from Kansas City in January. Name's Bubbles Caesar. That's not the straight handle, Carella. She was born Barbara Cesare, the Bubbles is for the stage. She's *got* them, too, believe me."

"Well, what about her?" Carella asked.

"She was reported missing by her agent, a guy named Charles Tudor, on February thirteenth, day before Valentine's Day. What's today's date, anyway?"

"The eleventh," Carella said.

"Yeah, that's right. Well, that makes it longer than three weeks. Anyway, we've been looking for her all this time, and checking up on her past history, all that. What we found out is this. She flew here from K.C."

"She did?"

"Yeah, and you can guess the rest. She flew with this

Circle Airlines. Now this can be sheer coincidence, or it can amount to something, I don't know. But I thought I'd pass it on."

"Yeah," Carella said.

"It's a long shot, I'll admit it. Only there may be a tie-in."

"How'd she fly?" Carella asked. "Luxury, Tourist?"

"First Class," Bartholdi said. "That's another thing. They give them little bags to First Class passengers, don't they?"

"Yeah," Carella said.

"Yeah. You know, this may be really far out, but suppose this dame vanished because she done some guy in? I mean, the hand *was* in a Circle Airlines . . ." Bartholdi let the sentence trail. "Well, I admit it's a long shot."

"We've run out of the other kind," Carella said. "What's Tudor's address?"

The Creo Building was situated in midtown Isola, smack on The Stem, and served as an unofficial meeting place for every musician and performer in town. The building was flanked by an all-night cafeteria and a movie house, and its wide entrance doors opened on a marble lobby which would not have seemed out of place in St. Peter's. Beyond the lobby, the upper stories of the building deteriorated into the lesser splendor of unfurnished rehearsal halls and the cubbyhole offices of music publishers, composers, agents, and an occasional ambulance chaser renting telephone and desk space. The men and women who congregated before the entrance doors and in the lobby were a mixed lot.

Here could be seen the hip musicians with the dizzy kicks and the tenor sax cases and the trombone cases discussing openings on various bands, some of them passing around sticks of marijuana, others lost in the religion that was music and needing no outside stimulation. Here, too, were the long-haired classicists carrying oboe cases, wearing soft felt hats, discussing the season in Boston or Dallas, and wondering whether Bernstein

would make it at the Philharmonic. Here were the wom-
en singers, the canaries, the thrushes whose grins were
as trained as their voices, who—no matter how minus-
cule the band they sang with—entered the arcade like
Hollywood movie queens.

Here were the ballet dancers and the modern dancers,
wearing short black skirts which permitted freer move-
ment, their high heels clicking on the marble floor,
walking with that peculiar duck waddle which seems to
be the stamp of all professional dancers. Here were the
strippers, the big pale women untouched by the sun,
wearing dark glasses and lipstick slashes. Here were the
publishers, puffing on cigars and looking like the Russian concept of the American capitalist. And here were
the unsuccessful composers, needing haircuts, and here
were the slightly successful composers carrying demo
records, and here were the really successful composers
who sang badly and who played piano more badly but
who walked with the cool assurance of jukebox loot
spilling out of their ears.

Upstairs, everybody was rehearsing, rehearsing with
small combos and big bands, rehearsing with pianos, rehearsing with drums, rehearsing dances and symphonies
and improvised jam sessions. The only thing that wasn't
rehearsed in the Creo Building was the dialogue going
on in the lobby and before the entrance doors.

The dialogue of Charles Tudor may or may not have
been rehearsed, it was difficult to tell. His small office
was on the eighteenth floor of the building. Two tall,
pale, buxom girls carrying hatboxes were sitting on a
wooden bench in the waiting room. A short, rosy-
cheeked, flat-chested girl was sitting behind a desk at the
far end of the room. Carella went to her, flashed the tin,
and said, "We're from the police. We'd like to talk to
Mr. Tudor, please."

The receptionist studied first Hawes, then Carella.
The two pale strippers on the bench turned a few shades
paler. The taller of the two rose abruptly, picked up her
hatbox, and hastily departed. The second busied herself
with a copy of *Variety*.

"What's this in reference to?" the receptionist asked.

"We'll discuss that with Mr. Tudor," Carella said. "Would you mind telling him we're here?"

The girl pulled a face and pressed a stud in the phone on her desk. "Mr. Tudor," she said into the mouthpiece, "there are a couple of gentlemen here who *claim* to be detectives. Well, they said they'd discuss that with you, Mr. Tudor. I couldn't say, I've never met a detective before. Yes, he showed me a badge. Yes, sir." She hung up.

"You'll have to wait a minute. He's got somebody with him."

"Thank you," Carella said.

They stood near the desk and looked around the small waiting room. The second stripper sat motionless behind her *Variety*, not even daring to turn the page. The walls of the room were covered with black-and-white photos of strippers in various provocative poses. Each of the photographs was signed. Most of them started with the words "To Charlie, who . . ." and ended with exotic names like Flame or Torch or Maja or Exota or Bali. Hawes walked around the room looking at the photos. The girl behind the copy of *Variety* followed him with her eyes.

Finally, in a very tiny voice which seemed even smaller issuing from such a big woman, she said, "That's me."

Hawes turned. "Huh?" he asked.

"With the furs. The picture you were looking at. It's me."

"Oh. Oh," Hawes said. He turned to look at the picture again. Turning back to the girl, he said, "I didn't recognize you with your . . ." and then stopped and grinned.

The girl shrugged.

"Marla? Is that your name? The handwriting isn't too clear."

"Marla, that's it," she said. "It's really Mary Lou, but my first agent changed it to Marla. That sounds exotic, don't you think?"

"Yes, yes, very," Hawes agreed.

"What's your name?"

"Hawes."

"That's all?"

"Well, no. Cotton is my first name. Cotton Hawes."

The girl stared at him for a moment. Then she asked, "Are *you* a stripper, too?" and burst out laughing. "Excuse me," she said, "but you have to admit that's a pretty exotic name."

"I guess so," Hawes said, grinning.

"Is Mr. Tudor in some trouble?" Marla asked.

"No." Hawes shook his head. "No trouble."

"Then why do you want to see him?"

"Why do *you* want to see him?" Hawes asked.

"To get a booking."

"Good luck," Hawes said.

"Thank you. He's a good agent. He handles a lot of exotic dancers. I'm sure he'll get me something."

"Good," Hawes said. "I hope so."

The girl nodded and was silent for a while. She picked up the copy of *Variety*, thumbed through it, and then put it down again. "You still haven't told me why you want to see Mr. Tudor," she said, and at that moment the door to the inner office opened and a statuesque brunette wearing heels which made her four inches taller stepped into the waiting room, bust first.

"Thanks a lot, Charlie," she yelled, almost colliding with Carella to whom she hastily said, "Oh, pardon me, dearie," and then clattered out of the room.

The phone on the receptionist's desk buzzed. She lifted the receiver. "Yes, Mr. Tudor," she said, and then hung up. "Mr. Tudor will see you now," she said to Carella.

"Good luck," Marla said to Hawes as he moved past the bench.

"Thank you," Hawes said. "The same to you."

"If I ever need a cop or something," she called after him, "I'll give you a ring."

"Do that," Hawes said, and he followed Carella into Tudor's office. The office was decorated with more photographs of exotic dancers, so many photographs that both Tudor and his desk were almost lost in the display. Tudor was a huge man in his late forties wearing a dark-brown suit and a pale-gold tie. He possessed a headful of short black hair which was turning white at the temples, and a black Ernie Kovacs mustache. He was smoking a cigarette in a gold-and-black cigarette holder. He gestured the detectives to chairs, and a diamond pinky ring glistened on his right hand.

"I understand you're policemen," he said. "Does this have anything to do with Barbara?"

"Yes, sir," Carella said. "We understand that you were the gentleman who reported Miss Caesar missing."

"Yes," Tudor said. "You must forgive my rudeness when my receptionist announced you. I sometimes get calls from policemen which have nothing whatever to do with . . . well, something as serious as Barbara."

"What kind of calls, Mr. Tudor?" Hawes asked.

"Oh, you know. A show is closed down someplace, and some of my girls are in it, and immediately the police make an association. I only find employment for these girls. I don't tell them how to observe the rules of propriety." Tudor shrugged. His speech was curious in that it was absolutely phony. He spoke with the clipped precision of an Englishman, and one received the impression that he chose his words carefully before allowing them to leave his mouth. But the elegant tones and rounded vowels were delivered in the harshest, most blatant city accent Carella had ever heard. And the odd part was that Tudor didn't seem at all aware of the accent that stamped him as a native of either Isola or Calm's Point. Blithely, he clipped his words immaculately and seemed under the impression that he was a member of the House of Lords delivering a speech to his fellow peers.

"I really am not responsible for whatever acts my clients wish to concoct," Tudor said. "I wish the police would realize that. I am a booking agent, not a choreog-

rapher." He smiled briefly. "About Barbara," he said.
"What have you heard?"

"Nothing at all, Mr. Tudor. We were hoping you
could tell us a little more about her."

"Oh."

Tudor uttered only that single word, but disappointment was evident in it, and disappointment showed immediately afterward on his face.

"I'm sorry if we raised your hopes, Mr. Tudor," Carella said.

"That's all right," Tudor said. "It's just . . ."

"She meant a lot to you, this girl?"

"Yes," Tudor answered. He nodded his head. "Yes."

"In a business way?" Hawes asked.

"Business?" Tudor shook his head again. "No, not
business. I've handled better strippers. *Am* handling better ones now. That little girl who just left my office. Her
name is Pavan, got here from Frisco last July and has
just about set this metropolis on fire. Excellent. Absolutely excellent, and she's only twenty years old, would
you believe it? She has a long future ahead of her, that
girl. Barbara was no child, you know."

"How old is she?"

"Thirty-four. Of course, there are strippers who keep
performing until they're well into their fifties. I don't
know of any performers, or of any *women* for that matter, who take as much pride in their bodies as exotic
dancers do. I suppose there's an element of narcissism
involved. Or perhaps we're looking too deep. They
know their bodies are their fortunes. And so they take
care of themselves. Barbara, though she was thirty-four,
possessed . . ." Tudor stopped short. "Forgive me. I
must get out of the habit of using the past tense in
speaking about her. It's simply that, when a person
leaves, disappears, that person is thought of as being
gone, and the tongue plays its trick. Forgive me."

"Are we to understand, Mr. Tudor, that there was
something more than a strict business relationship between you and Miss Caesar?"

"More?" Tudor said.

"Yes, was there . . ."

"I love her," Tudor said flatly.

The room was silent.

"I see," Carella said.

"Yes." Tudor paused for a long time. "I love her. I still love her. I must keep remembering that. I must keep remembering that I still love her, and that she is still here."

"Here?"

"Yes. Here. Somewhere. In this city. She is still here." Tudor nodded. "Nothing has happened to her. She is the same Barbara, laughing, lovely . . ." He stopped himself. "Have you seen her picture, gentlemen?"

"No," Carella said.

"I have some, I believe. Would they help you?"

"Yes, they would."

"I have already given some to the Missing Persons Bureau. Are you from the Missing Persons Bureau?"

"No."

"No, I didn't think you were. Then what is your interest in Barbara?"

"We're acting in an advisory capacity," Carella lied.

"I see." Tudor stood up. He seemed taller on his feet, a man bigger than six feet who walked with economy and grace to the filing cabinet in one corner of the room. "I think there are some in here," he said. "I usually have pictures taken as soon as I put a girl under contract. I had quite a few taken of Barbara when she first came to me."

"When was this, Mr. Tudor?"

Tudor did not look up from the files. His hands worked busily as he spoke. "January. She came here from Kansas City. A friend of hers in a show there recommended me to her. I was the first person she met in this city."

"She came to you first, is that correct, Mr. Tudor?"

"Straight from the airport. I helped her get settled. I fell in love with her the moment I saw her."

"Straight from the airport?" Carella asked.

"What? Yes. Ah, here are the pictures." He turned from the files and carried several glossy prints to his desk. "This is Barbara, gentlemen. Bubbles Caesar. Beautiful, isn't she?"

Carella did not look at the pictures. "She came straight from the airport, you say?"

"Yes. Most of these pictures . . ."

"Was she carrying any luggage?"

"Luggage? Yes, I believe so. Why?"

"What kind of luggage?"

"A suitcase, I believe. A large one."

"Anything else?"

"I don't remember."

"Was she carrying a small, blue overnight bag?" Hawes asked.

Tudor thought for a moment. "Yes, I think she was. One of those small bags the airlines give you. Yes, she was."

"Circle Airlines, Mr. Tudor?"

"I don't remember. I have the impression it was Pan American."

Carella nodded and picked up the photographs. The girl Barbara "Bubbles" Caesar did not seem to be thirty-four years old, not from the photographs, at any rate. The pictures showed a clear-eyed, smiling brunette lossely draped in what seemed to be a fisherman's net. The net did very little to hide the girl's assets. The girl had assets in abundance. And coupled with these was the provocative look that all strippers wore after they'd ceased to wear anything else. Bubbles Caesar looked out of the photographs with an expression that clearly invited trouble. Studying the photos, Carella was absolutely certain that this was the identical look which Eve had flashed at Adam after taking her midday fruit. The look spelled one thing and one thing alone and, even realizing that the look was an acquired one, a trick of the girl's trade, Carella studied the photos and found that his palms were getting wet.

"She's pretty," he said inadequately.

"The pictures don't do her justice," Tudor said. "She

has a complexion like a peach and . . . and a vibration that can only be sensed through knowing her. There are people who vibrate, gentlemen. Barbara is one of them."

"You said you helped her get settled, Mr. Tudor. What, exactly, did you do?"

"I got a hotel for her, to begin with. Until she found a place of her own. I advanced her some money. I began seeing her regularly. And, of course, I got a job for her."

"Where?"

"The King and Queen. It's an excellent club."

"Where's that, Mr. Tudor?"

"Downtown, in The Quarter. I've placed some very good girls there. Pavan started there when she came here from Frisco. But, of course, Pavan had big-time quality, and I moved her out very fast. She's working on The Street now. A place called The String of Pearls. Do you know it?"

"It sounds familiar," Carella said. "Miss Caesar was not big-time in your opinion, is that right?"

"No. Not bad. But not big-time."

"Despite those . . . vibrations."

"The vibrations were a part of her personality. Sometimes they come over on the stage, sometimes they don't. Believe me, if Barbara could have incorporated this . . . this inner glow into her act, she'd have been the biggest ever, the biggest. Bar none. Gypsy Rose Lee, Margie Hart, Zorita, Lili St. Cyr, I tell you Barbara would have outshone them all. But no." He shook his head. "She was a second-rate stripper. Nothing came across the footlights but that magnificent body and, of course, the look that all strippers wear. But not the glow, not the vibrations, not the . . . the life force, call it what you will. These only came from knowing her. There is a difference, you understand."

"Was she working at The King and Queen when she disappeared?"

"Yes. She didn't show up for the show on February twelfth. The owner of the club reported this to me as her agent, and I called her apartment. She was living at the time with two other girls. The one who answered the phone told me that she hadn't seen her since early that morning. I got alarmed, and I went out to look for her. This is a big city, gentlemen."

"Yes."

"The next morning, the thirteenth, I called the police." Tudor paused. He looked past the detectives and through the window where the rain dripped steadily against the red brick of the Creo Building. "I had bought her a necklace for Valentine's Day. I was going to give it to her on Valentine's Day." He shook his head. "And now she's gone."

"What kind of a necklace, Mr. Tudor?"

"A ruby necklace. She has black hair, you know, very black, and deep brown eyes. I thought rubies, I thought the fire of rubies . . ." He paused again. "But she's gone, isn't she?"

"Who owns The King and Queen, Mr. Tudor?"

"A man named Randy Simms. Randolph is his full name, I believe, but everyone calls him Randy. He runs a very clean establishment. Do you plan to call on him?"

"Yes. Maybe he can give us some help."

"Find her, would you?" Tudor said. "Oh, God, please find her."

Eleven

THE KING AND QUEEN was actually on the outermost fringe of The Quarter, really closer to the brownstone houses which huddled in the side streets off Hall Avenue than to the restaurants, coffee houses, small theaters and art shops which were near Canopy Avenue.

The place was a step-down club, its entrance being one step down from the pavement. To the right of the entrance doorway was a window which had been constructed of pieces of colored glass in an attempt to simulate a stained-glass window. The colored panes showed a playing-card portrait of a king on the left, and a playing-card portrait of a queen on the right. The effect was startling, lighted from within so that it seemed as if strong sunlight were playing on the glass. The effect, too, was dignified and surprising. Surprising because one expected something more blatant of a strip joint, the life-sized placards out front featuring an Amazonian doll in the middle of a bump or a grind. There were no placards outside this club. Nor was there a bold display of typography announcing the name of the place. A small, round, gold escutcheon was set off center in the entrance door, and this was the only indication of the club's name. The address—"12N."—was engraved onto another round gold plaque set in the lower half of the door.

Hawes and Carella opened the door and walked in.

The club had that same slightly tired, unused look that most night clubs had during the daytime. The look was always startling to Carella. It was as if one suddenly came across a middle-aged woman dressed in black sat-

in and wearing diamonds at ten o'clock in the morning
in Schrafft's. The King and Queen looked similarly ov-
erdressed and weary during the daylight hours, and perhaps more lonely. There wasn't a sign of life in the
place.

"Hello!" Carella called. "Anybody home?"

His voice echoed into the long room. A window at the
far end admitted a single gray shaft of rain-dimmed
light. Dust motes slid down the shaft of light, settled si-
lently on the bottoms of deserted chairs stacked on
round tables.

"Hello?" he called again.

"Empty," Hawes said.

"Looks that way. Anybody here?" Carella yelled
again.

"Who is it?" a voice answered. "We don't open until
six P.M."

"Where are you?" Carella shouted to the voice.

"In the kitchen. We're closed."

"Come on out here a minute, will you?"

A man appeared suddenly in the gloom, wiping his
hands on a dish towel. He stepped briefly into the narrow shaft of light and then walked to where the two detectives were standing.

"We're closed," he said.

"We're cops," Carella answered.

"We're still closed. Especially to cops. If I served you,
I'd get my liquor license yanked."

"You Randy Simms?" Hawes asked.

"That's me," Simms said. "Why? What'd I do?"

"Nothing. Can we sit down and talk someplace?"

"Anyplace," Simms said. "Choose your table."

They pulled chairs off one of the tables and sat.
Simms was a sandy-haired man in his late forties, wearing a white dress shirt open at the throat, the sleeves
rolled up. There was a faintly bored expression on his
handsome face. He looked like a man who spent his
summers at St. Tropez at home among the girls in the
bikinis, his winters at St. Moritz skiing without safety

bindings. Carella was willing to bet he owned a Mercedes-Benz and a collection of Oriental jade.

"What's this about?" Simms asked. "Some violation? I had the other doors put in, and I put up the occupancy signs. So what is it this time?"

"We're not firemen," Carella said. "We're cops."

"What difference does it make? Cops or firemen, whenever either of them come around, it costs me money. What is it?"

"You know a girl named Bubbles Caesar?"

"I do," Simms said.

"She work for you?"

"She used to work for me, yes."

"Any idea where she is?"

"Not the vaguest. Why? Did she do something?"

"She seems to have disappeared."

"Is that a crime?"

"Not necessarily."

"Then why do you want her?"

"We want to talk to her."

"You're not alone," Simms said.

"What do you mean?"

"Only that everybody who ever walked into this joint wanted to talk to Barbara, that's all. She's a very attractive girl. A pain in the ass, but very attractive."

"She gave you trouble?"

"Yes, but not in a professional sense. She always arrived on time, and she did her act when she was supposed to, and she was friendly with the customers, so there was no trouble that way."

"Then what way *was* there trouble?"

"Well, there were a couple of fights in here."

"Over Barbara?"

"Yes."

"Who?"

"What do you mean, who?"

"Who did the fighting?"

"Oh, I don't remember," Simms said. "Customers. It's a funny thing with strippers. A man watches a woman take off her clothes, and he forgets he's in a public place and that the girl is a performer. He enters a fantasy in which he is alone with this girl, and she's taking off her clothes only for *him*. Well, sometimes the fantasy persists after the lights go up. And when two guys share the same fantasy, there can be trouble. A man who thinks the girl belongs to *him*, is undressing for *him*, doesn't like the idea of another guy sharing the same impression. Bang, the fists explode. So we heave them out on the sidewalk. Or at least we did. No more now."

"Now you let them fight?" Hawes asked.

"No. Now we don't give them a chance to fantasize."

"How do you prevent that?"

"Simple. No strippers."

"Oh? Have you changed the club's policy?"

"Yep. No strippers, no band, no dancing. Just a high-class jazz pianist, period. Drinks, dim lights, and cool music. You bring your own broad, and you hold hands with *her*, not with some dame wiggling on the stage. We haven't had a fight in the past two weeks."

"What made you decide on this new policy, Mr. Simms?"

"Actually, Barbara had a lot to do with it. She provoked a lot of the fights. I think she did it purposely. She'd pick out two of the biggest guys in the audience, and split her act between them. First one guy, then the other. Afterwards, when she came out front, she'd play up to both of them, and bang, came the fists. Then she didn't show up for work one night, so I was left with a string of second-run strippers and no headliner. It looked like amateur night at The King and Queen. And the trouble with the band, believe me, it wasn't worth it."

"What kind of trouble with the band?"

"Oh, all kinds. One of the guys on the band was a hophead, the trombone player. So I never knew whether he was going to show up for work or be found puking in some gutter. And then the drummer took off without a word, just didn't show up one night. The drummer is a very important man in a band that accompanies strippers. So I was stuck without a headliner, and without a drummer. So you can imagine what kind of a show I had that night."

"Let me get this straight," Carella said. "Are you saying that Barbara and this drummer both disappeared at the same time?"

"The same night, yes."

"This was when?"

"I don't remember when exactly. A few days before Valentine's Day, I think."

"What was this drummer's name?"

"Mike something. An Italian name. A real tongue twister. I can't remember it. It started with a C."

"Were Barbara and Mike very friendly?"

"They didn't seem to be, no. At least, I never noticed anything going on between them. Except the usual patter that goes on between the girls in the show and the band. But nothing special. Oh, I see," Simms said. "You think they took off together, is that it?"

"I don't know," Carella said. "It's a possibility."

"Anything's possible with strippers and musicians," Simms agreed. "I'm better off without them, believe me. This piano player I've got now, he plays very cool music, and everybody sits and listens in the dark, and it's great. Quiet. I don't need fist fights and intrigue."

"You can't remember this drummer's last name."

"No."

"Try."

"It began with a C, that's all I can tell you. Italian names throw me."

"What was the name of the band?" Carella said.

"I don't think it had a name. It was a pickup band."

"It had a leader, didn't it?"

"Well, he wasn't exactly a leader. Not the type anybody would want to be taken to, if you follow me. He was just the guy who rounded up a bunch of musicians for the job."

"And what was his name?"

"Elliot. Elliot Chambers."

"One other thing, Mr. Simms," Carella said. "Barbara's

agent told us she was living with two other girls when she disappeared. Would you know who those girls were?"

"I know one of them," Simms said without hesitation. "Marla Phillips. She used to be in the show, too."

"Would you know where she lives?"

"She's in the book," Simms said. He paused and looked at the detectives. "Is that it?"

"That's it," Carella said.

Outside, Hawes said, "What do you make of it?"

Carella shrugged. "I'm going to check with the musician's local, see if I can't get a last name for this Mike the drummer."

"Do drummers have big hands?"

"Search me. But it looks like more than coincidence, doesn't it? Both of them taking a powder on the same night?"

"Yeah, it does," Hawes said. "What about Marla Phillips?"

"Why don't you drop in and pay a visit?"

"All right," Hawes said.

"See what a nice guy I am? I tackle the musicians union, and I leave the stripper to you."

"You're a married man," Hawes said.

"And a father," Carella added.

"*And* a father, that's right."

"If you need any help, I'll be back at the squad."

"What help could I possibly need?" Hawes asked.

Marla Phillips lived on the ground floor of a brownstone four blocks from The King and Queen. The name plate on the mailboxes listed a hyphenated combination of three names: Phillips-Caesar-Smith. Hawes rang the bell, waited for the responding buzz that opened the inner door, and then stepped into the hallway. The apartment was at the end of the hall. He walked to it, rang the bell set in the door jamb, and waited. The door opened almost instantly.

Marla Phillips looked at him and said, "Hey!"

He recognized her instantly, of course, and then wondered where his mind was today. He had made no connection with the name when Simms had first mentioned it.

"Aren't you the cop who was in Mr. Tudor's office?" Marla asked.

"That's me," he said.

"Sure. Cotton something. Well, come on in, Cotton. Boy, this is a surprise. I just got home a minute ago. You're lucky you caught me. I have to leave in about ten minutes. Come in, come in. You'll catch cold standing in the hallway."

Hawes went into the apartment. Standing next to Marla, he realized how tall she truly was. He tried to visualize her on a runway, but the thought was staggering. He followed her into the apartment instead.

"Don't mind the underwear all over the place," Marla said. "I live with another girl. Taffy Smith. She's an actress. Legit. Would you like a drink?"

"No, thank you," Hawes said.

"Too early, huh? Look, will you do me a favor?"

"Sure," Hawes said.

"I have to call my service to see if there was anything for me while I was out. Would you feed the cat, please? The poor thing must be starved half to death."

"The cat?"

"Yeah, he's a Siamese, he's wandering around here somewhere. He'll come running into the kitchen the minute he hears you banging around out there. The cat food is under the sink. Just open up a can and put some in his bowl. And would you heat some milk for him? He can't stand cold milk."

"Sure," Hawes said.

"You're a honey," she told him. "Go ahead now, feed him. I'll be with you in a minute."

She went to the telephone and Hawes went into the kitchen. As he opened the can of cat food under the watchful eyes of the Siamese who had materialized instantly, he listened to Marla in the other room.

"A Mr. Who?" she asked the telephone. "Well, I don't know anybody by that name, but I'll give him a

ring later in the afternoon. Anyone else? Okay, thank
you."

She hung up and walked into the kitchen.

"Are you still warming the milk?" she asked. "It'll be
too hot. You'd better take it off now." Hawes took off
the saucepan and poured the milk into the bowl on the
floor.

"Okay, now come with me," Marla said. "I have to
change, do you mind? I've got a sitting in about five
minutes. I do modeling on the side. Cheesecake, you
know. For the men's magazines. I've got to put on some
fancy lingerie. Come on, come on, please hurry. This
way."

He followed her into a bedroom that held two twin
beds, a huge dresser, several chairs, and an assortment
of soiled cardboard coffee containers, wooden spoons,
and clothing piled haphazardly on the floor and on the
top of every available surface.

"Forgive the mess," Marla said. "My roommate is a
slob." She took off her suit jacket and threw it on the
floor, slipping out of her pumps at the same time. She
began pulling her blouse out of her skirt and then said,
"Would you mind turning your back? I hate to be a
prude, but I am."

Hawes turned his back, wondering why Marla Phillips thought it perfectly all right to take off her clothes
in a night club before the eyes of a hundred men, but
considered it indecent to perform the same act in a bedroom before the eyes of a single man. *Women,* he
thought, and he shrugged mentally. Behind him, he
could hear the frantic swishing of cotton and silk.

"I hate garter belts," she said. "I'm a big girl. I need
something to hold me in. What's supposed to be so
damn sexy about a garter belt, anyway, would you mind
telling me? What was it you wanted, Cotton?"

"Somebody told us you used to room with Bubbles
Caesar. Is that right?"

"Yes, that's right. Oh, goddamn it, I've got a run."
She pushed past him half-naked, bent over to pull a pair
of stockings from the bottom drawer of the dresser, and

then vanished behind his back again. "Excuse me," she said. "What about Barbara?"

"Did she live with you?"

"Yes. Her name is still in the mailbox. There, that's better. Whenever I'm in a hurry, I tear stockings. I don't know what they make them out of these days. Tissue paper, I think. I'll have to take her name out, I suppose. When I get the time. Boy, if I only had time to do all the things I want to do. What about Barbara?"

"When did she move out?"

"Oh, you know. When there was that big fuss. When Mr. Tudor reported her missing and all."

"Around St. Valentine's Day."

"Yes, around that time."

"Did she tell you she was going?"

"No."

"Did she take her clothes with her?"

"No."

"Her clothes are still here?"

"Yes."

"Then she didn't really *move* out, she just never showed up again."

"Yes, but she'll probably be back. Okay, you can turn now."

Hawes turned. Marla was wearing a simple black dress, an offshade of black nylon stockings, and high-heeled black pumps. "Are my seams straight?" she asked.

"Yes, they seem perfectly straight."

"Do you like my legs? Actually, my legs are too skinny for the rest of me."

"They seem okay to me," Hawes said. "What makes you think Barbara will be back?"

"I have the feeling she's shacking up with somebody. She likes men, Barbara does. She'll be back. I guess that's why I really haven't taken her name out of the mailbox."

"These men she likes," Hawes said. "Was Mike the drummer one of them?"

"Not that I know of. At least, she never talked about

him or anything. And he never called here. Excuse me, I have to put on a new face."

She shoved Hawes aside and sat at the counter top before the large mirror. The counter was covered with cosmetics. Among the other jars and bottles, Hawes noticed a small jar labeled Skinglow. He picked it up and turned it over in his hands.

"This yours?" he asked.

"What?" Marla turned, lipstick brush in one hand. "Oh. Yes. Mine, *and* Taffy's, *and* Barbara's. We all use it. It's very good stuff. It doesn't fade out under the lights. Sometimes, under the lights, your body looks *too* white, do you know? It's all right to look white, but not ghostly. So we use the Skinglow, and it takes off the pallor. A lot of strippers and actresses use it."

"Do you know Mike's last name?"

"Sure. Chirapadano. It's a beaut, isn't it?"

"Does he have big hands?"

"All men have big hands," Marla said.

"I mean, did you notice that his hands were unusually large?"

"I never noticed. The only thing I noticed about that band was that they all had six hands."

"Mike included?"

"Mike included." She turned to him. "How do I look? What time is it?"

"You look fine. It's—" he glanced at his watch— "twelve-fifteen."

"I'm late," she said flatly. "Do I look sexy?"

"Yes."

"Well, okay then."

"Do you know any of the men Barbara saw?" Hawes asked. "Any she might run away with?"

"Well, there was one guy who called her an awful lot. Listen, I'm sorry I'm giving you this bum's rush act, but I really have to get out of here. Why don't you call me sometime? You're awfully cute. Or if you're in the neighborhood some night, drop in. She's always serving coffee, that goddamn screwy roommate of mine."

"I might do that," Hawes said. "Who was this person who called Barbara a lot?"

"Oh, what was his name? He sounded like a Russian or something. Just a minute," she said, "I'll think of it." She opened a drawer, took a black purse from it, and hastily filled it with lipstick, mascara, change, and a small woman's wallet. "There, that's that," she said. "Do I have the address? Yes." She paused. "Androvich, that was the name. Karl Androvich. A sailor or something. Look, Cotton, will you call me sometime? You're not married or anything, are you?"

"No. Did you say Androvich?"

"Yes. Karl Androvich. Will you call me? I think it might be fun. I'm not always in such a crazy rush."

"Well, sure, but . . ."

"Come on, I've got to go. You can stay if you want to, just slam the door on the way out, it locks itself."

"No, I'll come with you."

"Are you going uptown?"

"Yes."

"Good, we can share a cab. Come on, hurry. Would you like to come to the sitting? No, don't, I'll get self-conscious. Come on, come on. Slam the door! Slam the door, Cotton!"

He slammed the door.

"I'm wearing this black stuff that's supposed to be imported from France. The bra is practically nonexistent. These pictures ought to . . ."

"When did Androvich last call her?" Hawes asked.

"A few days before she took off," Marla said.

"There's a cab. Can you whistle?"

"Yes, sure, but . . ."

"Whistle!"

Hawes whistled. They got into the cab together.

"Oh, where the hell did I put that address?" Marla said. "Just a minute," she told the cabbie. "Start driving uptown on Hall, I'll have the address for you in a minute. Do you think she ran off with Androvich? Is that possible, Cotton?"

"I doubt it. Androvich is home. Unless . . ."

"Unless what?"

"I don't know. I guess we'll have to talk to Androvich."

"Here's the address," Marla said to the cabbie, "695 Hall Avenue. Would you hurry, please? I'm terribly late."

"Lady," the cabbie answered. "I have never carried a passenger in this vehicle who *wasn't* terribly late."

Twelve

AT THE SQUADROOM, Hawes told Carella, "I found out the drummer's name."

"So did I. I got Chambers' number from the union, and I called him. Drummer's name is Mike Chirapadano. I called the union back and got an address and telephone number for him, too."

"Call him yet?" Hawes asked.

"Yes. No answer. I'd like to stop by there later this afternoon. Have you had lunch yet?"

"No."

"Let's."

"Okay. We've got another stop to make, too."

"Where?"

"Androvich."

"What for? Lover Boy is back, isn't he?"

"Sure. But Bubbles' roomate told me Androvich was in the habit of calling her."

"The roommate?"

"No. Bubbles."

"Androvich? Androvich was calling Bubbles Caesar?"

"Uh-huh."

"So *he's* back in it again, huh?"

"It looks that way. He called her a few days before she vanished, Steve."

"Mmm. So what does that mean?"

"He's the only guy who would know, it seems to me."

"Yeah. Okay. Lunch first, then Chirapadano—Jesus, that *is* a tongue twister—and then our amorous sailor friend. Cotton, there are times when I get very very weary."

"Have you ever tried running a footrace with a stripper?" Hawes asked.

Mike Chirapadano lived in a furnished room on North Sixth. He was not in when the detectives dropped by, and his landlady told them he had not been around for the past month.

The landlady was a thin bird of a woman in a flowered housedress. She kept dusting the hallway while they spoke to her.

"He owes me almost two months' rent," she said. "Is he in some trouble?"

"When did you last see him, Mrs. Marsten?" Hawes asked.

"In Feb-uary," she answered. "He owes me for February, and he also owes me for March, if he's still living here. The way it looks to me, he ain't living here no more. Don't it look that way to you?"

"Well, I don't know. I wonder if we could take a look at his room."

"Sure. Don't make no nevermind to me. What's he done? He a dope fiend? All these musicians are dope fiends, you know."

"Is that right?" Carella asked as they walked upstairs.

"Sure. Main-liners. That means they shoot it right into their veins."

"Is that right?"

"Sure. It's poison, you know. That hero-in they shoot into their veins. That stuff. It's poison. His room is on the third floor. I was up there cleaning only yesterday."

"Is his stuff still up there?"

"Yep, his clothes and his drums, too. Now why would a man take off like that and leave his belongs behind? He must be a dope fiend is the only way I can figure it. Here, it's down the end of the hall. What did you say he done?"

"Would you know exactly when in February he left, Mrs. Marsten?"

"I would know exactly to the day," the landlady said, but she did not offer the information.

"Well, when?" Hawes asked.

"Feb-uary twelfth. It was the day before Friday the thirteenth, and that's how I remember. Friday the thirteenth, that's a hoodoo day if ever there was one. Here's his room. Just a second now, while I unlock the door."

She took a key from the pocket of her dress and fitted it into the keyhole. "There's something wrong with this lock; I have to get it fixed. There, that does it." She threw open the door. "Spic and span; I just cleaned it yesterday. Even picked up his socks and underwear from all over the floor. One thing I can't stand it's a sloppy-looking room."

They went into the room together.

"There's his drums over there by the window. The big one is the bass drum, and that round black case is what they call the snare. The other thing there is the high hat. All his clothes is still in the closet and his shaving stuff is in the bathroom, just the way he left them. I can't figure it, can you? What'd you say it was that he done?"

"Did you see him when he left, Mrs. Marsten?"

"No."

"How old a man is he?"

"He's just a young fellow, it's a shame the way these young fellows get to be main-liners and dope fiends, shooting all that there hero-in poison into their systems."

"How young, Mrs. Marten?"

"Twenty-four, twenty-five, no older than that."

"A big man?"

"More than six feet, I guess."

"Big hands?"

"What?"

"His hands. Were they big, did you notice?"

"I never noticed. Who looks at a man's hands?"

"Well, some women do," Carella said.

"All I know is he owes me almost two months' rent," Mrs. Marsten said, shrugging.

"Would you know whether or not he had a lot of girl friends, Mrs. Marsten? Did he ever bring a girl here?"

"Not to my house," the landlady said. "Not to my

house, mister! I don't allow any of that kind of stuff
here. No, sir. If he had girl friends, he wasn't fooling
around with them under my roof. I keep a clean house.
Both the rooms *and* the roomers."

"I see," Carella said. "You mind if we look around a
little?"

"Go right ahead. Call me when you're done, and I'll
lock the room. Don't make a mess. I just cleaned it yesterday."

She went out. Carella and Hawes stared at each other.

"Do you suppose they went to Kansas City, maybe?"
Hawes asked.

"I don't know. I'm beginning to wish both of them
went to hell. Let's shake down the room. Maybe he left
a clue."

He hadn't.

Karl Androvich was a mustached giant who could
have been a breathing endorsement for Marlboro cigarettes. He sat in a T-shirt at the kitchen table, his mus-
cles bulging bronze against the clean white, the tattoo
showing on his left biceps, "Meg" in a heart. His hair
was a reddish brown, and his mustache was a curious
mixture of red, brown and blond hairs, a carefully
trimmed, very elegant mustache which—reflecting its
owner's pride—was constantly touched by Androvich
during the course of the conversation. His hands were
immense. Every time they moved up to stroke the mustache, Carella flinched as if he were about to be hit.
Meg Androvich hovered about the kitchen, preparing
dinner, her ears glued to the conversation.

"There are a few things we'd like to know, Mr. Androvich," Carella said.

"Yeah, what's that?"

"To begin with, where were you between February
fourteenth and Monday when you came back to this
house?"

"That's my business," Androvich said. "Next question."

Carella was silent for a moment.

"Are you going to answer our questions here, Mr. Androvich, or shall we go up to the squadroom where you might become a little more talkative?"

"You going to use a rubber hose on me? Man, I've been worked over with a hose before. You don't scare me."

"You going to tell us where you were?"

"I told you that's my business."

"Okay, get dressed."

"What the hell for? You can't arrest me without a charge."

"I've got a whole bagful of charges. You're withholding information from the police. You're an accessory before a murder. You're . . ."

"A what? A murder? Are you out of your bloody mind?"

"Get dressed Androvich. I don't want to play around."

"Okay," Androvich said angrily. "I was on the town."

"On the town where?"

"Everywhere. Bars. I was drinking."

"Why?"

"I felt like it."

"Did you know your wife had reported you missing?"

"No. How the hell was I supposed to have known that?"

"Why didn't you call her?"

"What are you, a marriage counselor? I didn't feel like calling her, okay?"

"He didn't have to call me if he didn't feel like it," Meg said from the stove. "He's home now. Why don't you all leave him alone?"

"Keep out of this, Meg," Androvich warned.

"Which bars did you go to?" Hawes asked.

"I went all over the city. I don't remember the names of the bars."

"Did you go to a place called The King and Queen?"

"No."

"I thought you didn't remember the names."

"I don't."

"Then how do you know you *didn't* go to The King and Queen?"

"It doesn't sound familiar." A slight tic had begun in Androvich's left eye.

"Does the name Bubbles Caesar sound familiar?"

"No."

"Or Barbara Cesare?"

"No," Androvich answered, the muscle of his eye jerking.

"How about Marla Phillips?"

"Never heard of her."

"How about this phone number, Androvich? Sperling 7-0200. Mean anything to you?"

"No." The eye muscle was twitching wildly now.

"Mrs. Androvich," Carella said, "I think you'd better leave the room."

"Why?"

"We're about to pull out a few skeletons. Go on in the other room."

"My wife can hear anything you've got to say," Androvich said.

"Okay. Sperling 7-0200 is the telephone number of three girls who share an apartment. One of them is named . . ."

"Go on in the other room, M-M-Meg," Androvich said.

"I want to stay here."

"Do what I t-t-tell you to do."

"Why is he asking you about that phone number? What have you got to do with those three . . . ?"

"G-G-Get the hell in the other room, Meg, before I slap you silly. Now do what I say!"

Meg Androvich stared at her husband sullenly, and then went out of the kitchen.

"Damn S-S-S-Southern t-t-trash," Androvich muttered under his breath, the stammering more marked now, the tic beating at the corner of his eye.

"You ready to tell us a few things, Androvich?"

"Okay. I knew her."

"Bubbles?"

"Bubbles."

"How well did you know her?"

"Very well."

"How well is that, Androvich?"

"You want a d-d-diagram?"

"If you've got one."

"We were making it together. Okay?"

"Okay. When did you last see her?"

"February twelfth."

"You remember the date pretty easily."

"I ought to."

"What does that mean?"

"I . . . look, what the hell d-d-difference does all this make? The last time I saw her was on the t-t-twelfth. Last month. I haven't seen her since."

"You sure about that?"

"I'm positive."

"You sure you haven't been with her all this time?"

"I'm sure. Man, I wish I had been her. I was *supposed* . . ." Androvich cut himself off.

"Supposed to do what?" Hawes asked.

"N-N-Nothing."

"You called her on the twelfth after your ship docked, is that right?"

"Yes."

"And you saw her afterwards?"

"Yes, but only for about a half-hour or so."

"That morning?"

"No. It was in the afternoon."

"Where'd you see her?"

"At her p-p-p-place."

"Was anybody else there? Either of her roommates?"

"No. I never met her roommates."

"But you spoke to them on the telephone?"

"Yeah. I spoke to one of them."

"Marla Phillips?"

"I d-d-don't know which one it was."

"Did you speak to the roommate on the morning of the twelfth?"

"Yeah. I spoke to her, and then she called B-B-Bubbles to the phone."

"And then you went to the apartment that afternoon, right?"

"Right. For a half-hour."

"And then what?"

"Then I left. One of the r-r-r-roommates was supposed to be coming back. That d-d-damn place is like the middle of Main Street."

"And you haven't seen her since that afternoon?"

"That's right."

"Have you tried to contact her?"

Androvich hesitated. Then he said, "No."

"How come?"

"I just haven't. I figure she must have gone back to Kansas City."

"What makes you figure that?"

"I just figure. She isn't around, is she?"

"How do you know?"

"Huh?"

"If you haven't tried contacting her, how do you know she isn't around?"

"Well, m-m-maybe I did try to reach her once or twice."

"When?"

"I don't remember. During the past few weeks."

"And you couldn't reach her?"

"No."

"Who did you reach?"

"The g-g-goddamn answering service."

"Now, let's go back a little, Androvich. You said you visited Miss Caesar in her apartment on the afternoon of the twelfth. All right, why?"

"I wanted to talk to her."

"What about?"

"Various things."

"Like what? Come on, Androvich, let's stop the teeth-pulling!"

"What d-d-difference does it make to you guys?"

"It may make a lot of difference. Miss Caesar has disappeared. We're trying to find her."

"You're telling me she's disappeared! Boy, has she disappeared! Well, I d-d-don't know where she is. If I did know . . ." Again, he cut himself off.

"If you did know, then what?"

"Nothing."

"What did you talk about that afternoon?"

"Nothing."

"You spent a half-hour talking about nothing, is that right?"

"That's right."

"Did you go to bed with her that afternoon?"

"No. I told you her r-r-roommate was expected back."

"So you just sat and looked at each other, right?"

"More or less."

"Get dressed, Androvich. We're going to have to take a little ride."

"Ride, my ass! I don't know anything about where she is, dammit! If I knew, do you think I'd . . ."

"What? Finish it, Androvich! Say what you've got to say!"

"Do you think I'd be here? Do you think I'd be playing hubby and wifey with that mealy-mouthed hunk of Southern garbage? Do you think I'd be listening to this molasses dribble day in and day out? Kahl, honeh, cain't we-all go back t'Atlanta, honeh? Cain't we, Kahl? Do you think I'd be here listening to that crap if I knew where Bubbles was?"

"What would you be doing, Androvich?"

"I'd be with her, goddamnit! Where do you think I spent the last month?"

"Where?"

"Looking for her. Searching this city, every c-c-corner of it. Do you know how big this city is?"

"We've got some idea."

"Okay, I p-p-picked through it like somebody looking through a scalp for lice. And I didn't find her. And if I couldn't find her, she isn't here, believe me, because I covered every place, *every* place. I went to places you guys have never even heard of, l-l-looking for that broad. She's gone."

"She was that important to you, huh?"

"Yeah, she was that important to me."

Androvich fell silent. Carella stared at him.

"What did you talk about that afternoon, Karl?" he asked gently.

"We made plans," Androvich said. His voice was curiously low now. The tic had stopped suddenly. The stammer had vanished. He did not look up at the detectives. He fastened his eyes on his big hands, and he twisted those hands in his lap, and he did not look up.

"What kind of plans?"

"We were going to run away together."

"Where?"

"Miami."

"Why there?"

"She knew of a job she could get down there. In one of the clubs. And Miami's a big port. Not as big as this city, but big enough. I could always get work out of Miami. Or maybe I could get a job on one of the yachts. Anyway, we figured Miami was a good place for us."

"When were you supposed to leave?"

"Valentine's Day."

"Why then?"

"Well, my ship was pulling out on the fourteenth, so we figured that would give us a head start. We figured Meg would think I was in South America, and then by the time she realized I wasn't, she wouldn't know where the hell I was. That was the way we figured it."

"But instead, the chief officer called here to find out where you were."

"Yeah, and Meg reported me missing."

"Why *aren't* you in Miami, Karl? What happened?"

"She didn't show."

"Bubbles?"

"Yeah. I waited at the train station all morning. Then I called her apartment, and all I got was the goddamn answering service. I called all that day, and all that day I got that answering service. I went down to The King and Queen, and the bartender there told me she hadn't showed up for work the past two nights. That was when I began looking for her."

"Did you plan to marry this girl, Karl?"

"Marry her? How could I do that? I'm already married. Bigamy is against the law."

"Then what did you plan to do?"

"Just have fun, that's all. I'm a young guy. I deserve a little fun, don't I? Miami is a good town for fun."

"Do you think she could have gone to Miami without you?"

"I don't think so. I wired the club she mentioned, and they said she hadn't showed up. Besides, why would she do that?"

"Women do funny things."

"Not Bubbles."

"We'd better check with the Miami cops, Steve," Hawes said. "And maybe a teletype to Kansas City, huh?"

"Yeah." He paused and looked at Androvich. "You think she isn't here any more, huh? You think she's left the city?"

"That's the way I figure it. I looked everywhere. She couldn't be here. It'd be impossible."

"Maybe she's hiding," Carella said. "Maybe she did something and doesn't want to be found."

"Bubbles? No, not Bubbles."

"Ever hear of a man called Mike Chirapadano?"

"No. Who's he?"

"A drummer."

"I never heard of him."

"Bubbles ever mention him?"

"No. Listen, she ain't in this city, that much I can tell you. She just ain't here. Nobody can hide that good."

"Maybe not," Carella said. "But maybe she's here, anyway."

"What sense does that make? If she ain't out in the open, and she ain't hiding, what does that leave?"

"The river," Carella said.

Thirteen

IT STOPPED RAINING that Thursday.

Nobody seemed to notice the difference.

It was strange. For the past nine days, it had rained steadily and everyone in the city talked about the rain. There were jokes about building arks and jokes about the rain hurting the rhubarb, and it was impossible to go anywhere or do anything without someone mentioning the rain.

On Thursday morning, the sun came out. There was no fanfare of trumpets heralding the sun's appearance, and none of the metropolitan dailies shrieked about it in four-point headlines. The rain just went, and the sun just came, and everyone in the city trotted about his business as if nothing had happened. The rain had been with them too long. It had become almost a visiting relative whose departure is always promised but never really expected. At last, the relative had left and—as with most promised things in life—there was no soaring joy accompanying the event. If anything, there was almost a sense of loss.

Even the bulls of the 87th who quite naturally detested legwork in the rain did not greet the sun with any noticeable amount of enthusiasm.

They had got their teletypes out to Miami and Kansas City, and they had received their answering teletypes, and the answering teletypes told them that Barbara "Bubbles" Caesar was not at the moment gainfully employed in any of the various clubs in either of the cities. This did not mean that she wasn't living in either of the cities. It simply meant she wasn't working.

It was impossible to check bus or train transportation, but a call to every airline servicing both of the cities revealed that neither Bubbles Caesar nor a Mike Chirapadano had reserved passage out of Isola during the past month.

On Thursday afternoon, the Federal Bureau of Investigation delivered a photostatic copy of Mike Chirapadano's service record.

He had been born in Riverhead twenty-three years ago. He was white, and he was obviously male. Height, six feet three inches. Weight, 185. Eyes, blue. Hair, brown. When the Korean War broke out, he was only thirteen years old. When it ended, he was sixteen, and so he had been spared the Oriental bout. He had joined the Navy for a two-year hitch in July of 1956, had spent all of his service career—except for his boot training at the Great Lakes Naval Station—playing with the ComServDiv band in Miami. When he got out of the navy in 1958, he came back to Isola. His record listed an honorable discharge in Miami, the Navy providing his transportation back to his home city. A copy of his fingerprint record was included in the data from the FBI but the prints were worthless for comparison purposes since the fingertips on both discovered hands had been mutilated. The Navy listed his blood as belonging to the "O" group.

Carella studied the information and went home to his wife.

Teddy Carella was a deaf mute.

She was not a tall woman but she somehow managed to give the impression of height—a woman with black hair and brown eyes and a figure which, even after the bearing of twin children, managed to evoke street-corner whistles that that—unfortunately—Teddy could not hear.

The twins, Mark and April, had been born on a Sunday in June. June 22, to be exact. Carella would never forget the date because, aside from it being the day on which he'd been presented with two lovely children, it had also been the day of his sister Angela's wedding, and there had been quite a bit of excitement on that day, what with a sniper trying to pick off the groom and all. Happily, the groom had survived. He had survived very well. Angela, less than a year after her marriage, was already pregnant.

Now the problems of the care and feeding of twins are manifold even for a mother who possesses the powers of speech and hearing. The feeding problem is perhaps the least difficult because the eventuality of twins was undoubtedly considered in the design of the female apparatus and allowances made therefor. For which, thank God. But any mother who has tried to cope with the infantile madness of even one child must surely recognize that the schizophrenic rantings of twins present a situation exactly doubled in potential frenzy.

When Steve Carella discovered that his wife was pregnant, he was not exactly the happiest man in the world. His wife was a deaf mute. Would the children be similarly afflicted? He was assured that his wife's handicap was not an inherited trait, and that in all probability a woman as healthy in all other respects as Teddy would deliver an equally healthy baby. He had felt somewhat ashamed of his doubts later. In all truth, he never really considered Teddy either "handicapped" or "afflicted." She was, to him, the most beautiful and desirable woman on the face of the earth. Her eyes, her face, spoke more words to him than could be found in the languages of a hundred different nations. And when he spoke, she heard him, she heard him with more than ears, she heard him with her entire being. And so he'd felt some guilt at his earlier unhappiness, a guilt which slowly dissipated as the time of the birth drew near.

But he was not expecting twins, and when he was informed that he was now the father of a boy and a girl, the boy weighing in at six pounds four ounces, the girl being two ounces lighter than her brother, all of his old fears and anxieties returned. The fears became magnified when he visited the hospital the next morning and was told by the obstetrician that the firstborn, Mark, had broken his collarbone during delivery and that the doctor was placing him in an incubator until the collarbone healed. Apparently, the birth had been a difficult one and Mark had gallantly served as a trailblazer for his wombmate, suffering the fractured clavicle in his progress toward daylight. As it turned out, the fracture was simply a chipped bone, and it healed very rapidly, and the babies Carella and Teddy carried home from the hospital ten days later were remarkably healthy; but Carella was still frightened.

How will we manage? he wondered. How will Teddy manage to feed them and take care of them? How will they learn to speak? Wasn't speech a process of imitation? Oh, God, what will we do?

The first thing they had to do, they discovered, was to move. The Riverhead apartment on Dartmouth Road seemed to shrink the moment the babies and their nurse were put into the place. The nurse had been a gift from Teddy's father, a month's respite from the task of getting a household functioning again. The nurse was a marvelous woman in her fifties named Fanny. She had blue hair and she wore pincenez and she weighed a hundred and fifty pounds and she ran that house like an Army sergeant. She took an instant liking to Carella and his wife, and her fondness for the twins included such displays of affection as the embroidering of two pillow slips with their names, action clearly above and beyond the call of duty.

Whenever Carella had a day off, he and Teddy went looking for a house. Carella was a Detective 2nd/Grade and his salary—before the various deductions which decimated it—was exactly $5,555 a year. That is not a lot of loot. They had managed to save over the past years the grand total of two thousand bucks, and they were rapidly discovering that this paltry sum could barely cover the down payment on a lawn mower, much less a full-fledged house. For the first time in his life, Carella felt completely inadequate. He had brought two children into the world, and now he was faced with the possibility of being unable to house them properly, to give them the things they needed. And suddenly the Carellas discovered that their luck, by George, she was running good!

They found a house that could be had simply by paying the back taxes on it, which taxes amounted to ten thousand dollars. The house was a huge rambling monster in Riverhead, close to Donnegan's Bluff, a house which had undoubtedly held a large family and an army of servants in the good old days. These were the bad new days, however, and with servants and fuel costs being what they were, no one was very anxious to take over a white elephant like this one. Except the Carellas.

They arranged a loan through the local bank (a civil service employee is considered a good risk) and less than a month after the twins were born, they found themselves living in a house of which Charles Addams would have been ecstatically proud. Along about this time, their second stroke of good luck presented itself. Fanny, who had helped them move and helped them get settled, was due to terminate her month's employment when she offered the Carellas a proposition. She had, she told them, been making a study of the situation in the Carella household, and she could not visualize poor little Theodora (these were Fanny's words) raising those two infants alone, nor did she understand how the children were to learn to talk if they could not imitate their mother, and how was Theodora to hear either of the infants yelling, suppose one of them got stuck with a safety pin or something, my God?

Now she understood that a detective's salary was somewhere around five thousand a year—"You *are* a 2nd/grade detective, aren't you, Steve?"—and that such a salary did not warrant a full-time nurse and governess. But at the same time, she had the utmost faith that Carella would eventually make 1st/grade— "That *does* pay six thousand a year, doesn't it, Steve?"—and until the time when the Carellas could afford to pay her a decent wage, she would be willing to work for room and board, supplementing this with whatever she could earn making night calls and the like.

The Carellas would not hear of it.

She was, they insisted, a trained nurse, and she would be wasting her time by working for the Carellas at what

amounted to no salary at all when she could be out
earning a damned good living. And besides, she was not
a truck horse, how could she possibly work all day long
with the children and then hope to take on odd jobs at
night? No, they would not hear of it.

But neither would Fanny hear of their not hearing of
it.

"I am a very strong woman," she said, "and all I'll be
doing all day long is taking care of the children under
the supervision of Theodora who is their mother. I
speak English very well, and the children could do
worse for someone to imitate. And besides, I'm fifty-
three years old, and I've never had a family of my own,
and I rather like this family and so I think I'll stay. And
it'll take a bigger man than you, Steve Carella, to throw
me into the street. So that settles that."

And, indeed, that did settle that.

Fanny had stayed. The Carellas had sectioned off one
corner of the house and disconnected the heating to it so
that their fuel bills were not exorbitant. Slowly but
surely, the bank loan was being paid off. The children
were almost a year old and showed every sign of being
willing to imitate the sometimes colorful speech of their
nurse. Fanny's room was on the second floor of the
house, near the children's room, and the Carellas slept
downstairs in a bedroom off the living room so that
even their sex life went uninterrupted after that grisly
six-weeks' postnatal wait. Everything was rosy.

But sometimes a man came home looking for an argument, and you can't very well argue with a woman
who cannot speak. There are some men who might
agree that such a state of matrimony is surely a state approaching paradise, but on that Thursday night, with the
sky peppered with stars, with a springlike breeze in the
air, Carella walked up the path to the old house bristling
for a fight.

Teddy greeted him at the doorway. He kissed her
briefly and stamped into the house, and she stared after
him in puzzlement and then followed him.

"Where's Fanny?" he asked.

He watched Teddy's fingers as they rapidly told him, in sign language, that Fanny had left early for a nursing job.

"And the children?" he asked.

She read his lips, and then signaled that the children were already in bed, asleep.

"I'm hungry," he said. "Can we eat, please?"

They went into the kitchen, and Teddy served the meal—pork chops, his favorite. He picked sullenly at his food, and after dinner he went into the living room, turned on the television set, watched a show featuring a private eye who was buddy-buddy with a police lieutenant and who was also buddy-buddy with at least eighteen different women of assorted provocative shapes, and then snapped off the show and turned to Teddy and shouted, "If any police lieutenant in the country ran his squad the way that jerk does, the thieves would overrun the streets! No wonder he needs a private eye to tell him what to do!"

Teddy stared at her husband and said nothing.

"I'd like to see what the pair of them would do with a real case. I'd like to see how they'd manage without a dozen clues staring them in the face."

Teddy rose and went to her husband, sitting on the arm of his chair.

"I'd like to see what they'd do with a pair of goddamn severed hands. They'd probably both faint dead away," Carella said.

Teddy stroked his hair.

"We're back to Androvich again," he shouted. It occurred to him that it didn't matter whether or not he shouted because Teddy was only reading his lips and the decibels didn't matter one little damn. But he shouted nonetheless. "We're right back to Androvich, and where does that leave us? You want to know where that leaves us?"

Teddy nodded.

"Okay. We've got a pair of hands belonging to a white male who is somewhere between the ages of eighteen and twenty-four. We've got a bum of a sailor who flops down with any girl he meets, bong, bong, there goes Karl Androvich, who allegedly made a date to run off with a stripper named Bubbles Caesar. You listening?"

Yes, Teddy nodded.

"So they set the date for Valentine's Day, which is very romantic. All the tramps of the world are always very romantic. Only this particular tramp didn't show up. She left our sailor friend Androvich waiting in the lurch." He saw the frown on Teddy's face. "What's the matter? You don't like my calling Bubbles a tramp? She reads that way to me. She's provoked fights in the joint where she stripped by leading on two men simultaneously. She had this deal going with Androvich, and she also probably had something going with a drummer named Mike Chirapadano. At any rate, she and Chirapadano vanished on exactly the same day, so that stinks of conspiracy. And she's also got her agent, a guy named Charlie Tudor, all butterflies in the stomach over her. So it seems to me she was playing the field in six positions. And if that doesn't spell tramp, it comes pretty close."

He watched his wife's fingers as she answered him.

He interrupted, shouting, "What do you mean, maybe she's just a friendly girl? We know she was shacking up with the sailor, and probably with the drummer, and probably with the agent as well. All big men, too. She goes for them big. A tramp with . . ."

The drummer and the agent are only supposition, Teddy spelled with her hands. *The only one you have any sure knowledge of is the sailor.*

"I don't need any sure knowledge. I can read Bubbles Caesar from clear across the bay on a foggy day."

I thought sure knowledge was the only thing a detective used.

"You're thinking of a lawyer who never asks a question unless he's sure of what the answer will be. I'm not a lawyer, I'm a cop. I have to ask the questions."

Then ask them, and stop assuming that all strippers are . . .

Carella interrupted her with a roar that almost woke

the children. "Assuming! Who's assuming?" he bellowed, finally involved in the argument he'd been seeking ever since he came home, a curious sort of argument in that Teddy's hands moved unemotionally, filled with words, while he yelled and ranted to her silent fingers. "What does a girl have to do before I figure her for rotten? For all I know, she knocked off this guy Chirapadano and won't be happy until she's dropped his hands and his legs and his heart and his liver into the little paper sacks all over town! I won't be surprised if she cuts off his . . ."

Don't be disgusting, Steve, Teddy cautioned with her hands.

"Where the hell is she? That's what I'd like to know," Carella said. "And where's Chirapadano? And whose damn hands are those? And where's the rest of the body? And what's the motive in this thing? There had to be a motive, doesn't there? People just don't go around killing other people, do they?"

You're the detective. You tell me.

"There's always a motive," Carella said, "that's for sure. Always. Dammit, if we only *knew* more. Did Bubbles and the drummer go off together? Did she dump the sailor because she wanted the drummer? And if so, did she get tired of him and knock him off? Then why cut off his hands, and where's the rest of the body? And if they aren't his hands, then whose are they? Or are Bubbles and the drummer even connected with the hands? Maybe we're off on a wild goose chase altogether. Boy, I wish I was a shoemaker."

You do not wish you were a shoemaker, Teddy told him.

"Don't tell me what I wish," Carella said. "Boy, you're the most argumentive female I've ever met in my life. Come here and kiss me before we start a real fight. You've been looking for one ever since I got home."

And Teddy, smiling, went into his arms.

Fourteen

THE VERY NEXT DAY, Carella got the fight he was spoiling for.

Oddly, the fight was with another cop.

This was rather strange because Carella was a fairly sensible man who realized how much his colleagues could contribute to his job. He had certainly avoided any trouble on the squad prior to this, so it could only be assumed that the Hands Case—as the men had come to call it—was really getting him down.

The fight started very early in the morning, and it was one of those fights which seem to come about full-blown, with nothing leading up to them, like a summer storm which suddenly blackens the streets with rain. Carella was putting a call in to Taffy Smith, the other girl who'd shared the apartment with Bubbles Caesar. He mused that this damned case was beginning to resemble the cases of television's foremost private eye, with voluptuous cuties popping out of the woodwork wherever a man turned. He could not say he objected to the female pulchritude. It was certainly a lot more pleasant than investigating a case at an old ladies' home. At the same time, all these broads seemed to be leading nowhere, and it was this knowledge which rankled in him, and which probably led to the fight.

Hernandez was sitting at the desk alongside Carella's, typing a report. Sunshine sifted through the grilled windows and threw a shadowed lacework on the squadron floor. The door to Lieutenant Byrnes' office was open. Someone had turned on the standing electric fan, not

because it was really hot but only because the sunshine
—after so much rain—created an illusion of heat.

"Miss Smith?" Carella said into the phone.

"Yes. Who's this, please?"

"Detective Carella of the 87th Detective Squad."

"Oh, my goodness," Taffy Smith said.

"Miss Smith, we'd like to talk to you about your missing roommate, Bubbles Caesar. Do you suppose we
could stop by sometime today?"

"Oh. Well, gee, I don't know. I'm supposed to go to
rehearsal."

"What time is your rehearsal, Miss Smith?"

"Eleven o'clock."

"And when will you be through?"

"Gee, that's awfully hard to say. Sometimes they last
all day long. Although maybe this'll be a short one. We
got an awful lot done yesterday."

"Can you give me an approximate time?"

"I'd say about three o'clock. But I can't be sure.
Look, let's say three, and you can call here before you
leave your office, okay? Then if I'm delayed or anything, my service can give you the message. Okay?
Would that be okay?"

"That'd be fine."

"Unless you want me to leave the key. Then you
could go in and make yourself a cup of coffee. Would
you rather do that?"

"No, that's all right."

"Okay, then, I'll see you at three, okay?"

"Fine," Carella said.

"But be sure to call first, okay? And if I can't make
it, I'll leave a message. Okay?"

"Thank you, Miss Smith," Carella said, and he hung
up.

Andy Parker came through the slatted rail divider
and threw his hat at his desk. "Man, what a day," he
said. "Supposed to hit seventy today. Can you imagine
that? In March? I guess all that rain drove winter clear
out of the city."

"I guess so," Carella said. He listed the appointment

with Taffy on his pad and made a note to call her at 2:30 before leaving the squadroom.

"This is the kind of weather you got back home, hey, Chico?" Parker said to Hernandez.

Frankie Hernandez, who'd been typing, did not hear Parker. He stopped the machine, looked up, and said, "Huh? You talking to me, Andy?"

"Yeah. I said this is the kind of weather you got back home, ain't it?"

"Back home?" Hernandez said. "You mean Puerto Rico?"

"Sure."

"I was born here," Hernandez said.

"Sure, I know," Parker said. "Every Puerto Rican you meet in the streets, he was born here. To hear them tell it, none of them ever came from the island. You'd never know there was a place called Puerto Rico, to hear them tell it."

"That's not true, Andy," Hernandez said gently. "Most Puerto Ricans are very proud to have come from the island."

"But not you, huh? You deny it."

"I don't come from the island," Hernandez said.

"No, that's right. You were born here, right?"

"That's right," Hernandez said, and he began typing again.

Hernandez was not angry, and Parker didn't seem to be angry, and Carella hadn't even been paying any attention to the conversation. He was making out a tentative schedule of outside calls which he hoped he and Hawes could get to that day. He didn't even look up when Parker began speaking again.

"So that makes you an American, right, Chico?" Parker said.

This time, Hernandez heard him over the noise of the typewriter. This time, he looked up quickly and said, "You talking to me?" But whereas the words were exactly the words he'd used the first time Parker had spoken, Hernandez delivered them differently this time, delivered them with a tightness, an intonation of unmistakable annoyance. His heart had begun to pound furiously. He knew that Parker was calling upon him to defend The Cause once more, and he did not particularly feel like defending anything on a beautiful morning like this one, but the gauntlet had been dropped, and there it lay, and so Hernandez hurled back his words.

"You talking to me?"

"Yes, I am talking to you, Chico," Parker said. "It's amazing how you damn people never hear anything when you don't want to hear . . ."

"Knock it off, Andy," Carella said suddenly.

Parker turned toward Carella's desk. "What the hell's the matter with you?" he said.

"Knock it off, that's all. You're disturbing my squadroom."

"When the hell did this become *your* squadroom?"

"I'm catching today, and it looks like your name isn't even listed on the duty chart. So why don't you go outside and find some trouble in the streets, if trouble is what you want?"

"When did you become the champion of the people?"

"Right this minute," Carella said, and he shoved back his chair and stood up to face Parker.

"Yeah?" Parker said.

"Yeah," Carella answered.

"Well, you can just blow it out your . . ."

And Carella hit him.

He did not know he was going to throw the punch until after he had thrown it, until after it had collided with Parker's jaw and sent him staggering backward against the railing. He knew then that he shouldn't have hit Parker, but at the same time he told himself he didn't feel like sitting around listening to Hernandez take a lot of garbage on a morning like this, and yet he knew he shouldn't have thrown the punch.

Parker didn't say a word. He shoved himself off the railing and lunged at Carella who chopped a short right to Parker's gut, doubling him over. Parker grabbed for his midsection and Carella delivered a rabbit punch to the back of Parker's neck, sending him sprawling over the desk.

Parker got up and faced Carella with new respect and with renewed malice. It was as if he'd forgotten for a moment that his opponent was as trained and as skilled as he himself was, forgotten that Carella could fight as clean or as dirty as the situation warranted, and that the situation generally warranted the dirtiest sort of fighting, and that this sort of fighting had become second nature.

"I'm gonna break you in half, Steve," Parker said, and there was almost a chiding tone in his voice, the tone of warning a father uses to a child who is acting up.

He feinted with his left and as Carella moved to dodge the blow, he slammed a roundhouse right into his nose, bringing blood to it instantly. Carella touched his nose quickly, saw the blood, and then brought up his guard.

"Cut it out, you crazy bastards," Hernandez said, stepping between them. "The skipper's door is open. You want him to come out here?"

"Sure. Steve-oh doesn't care, do you, Steve? You and the skipper are real buddies, aren't you?"

Carella dropped his fists. Angrily, he said, "We'll finish this another time, Andy."

"You're damn right we will," Parker said, and he stormed out of the squadroom.

Carella took a handkerchief from his back pocket and began dabbing at his nose. Hernandez put a cold key at the back of his neck.

"Thanks, Steve," he said.

"Don't mention it," Carella answered.

"You shouldn't have bothered. I'm used to Andy."

"Yeah, but I guess I'm not."

"Anyway, thanks."

Hawes walked into the squadroom, saw Carella's bloody handkerchief, glanced hastily at the lieutenant's door, and then whispered, "What happened?"

"I saw red," Carella said.

Hawes glanced at the handkerchief again. "You're *still* seeing red," he said.

Taffy Smith was neither voluptuous, overblown, *zoftik,* nor even pretty. She was a tiny little girl with ash blond hair trimmed very close to her head. She had the narrow bones of a sparrow, and a nose covered with freckles, and she wore harlequin glasses which shielded the brightest blue eyes Carella or Hawes had ever seen.

There was, apparently, great Freudian meaning to this girl's penchant for making coffee for strangers. Undoubtedly, as a child, she had witnessed her mother clobbering her father with a coffeepot. Or perhaps a pot of coffee had overturned, scalding her, and she now approached it as a threat to be conquered. Or perhaps she had been raised by a tyrannical aunt in Brazil where, so the song says, coffee beans grow by the millions. Whatever the case, she trotted into the kitchen and promptly got a pot going while the detectives sat down in the living room. The Siamese cat, remembering Hawes, sidled over to him and purred idiotically against his leg.

"Friend of yours?" Carella asked.

"I fed him once," Hawes answered.

Taffy Smith came back into the living room. "Gee, I'm bushed," she said. "We've been rehearsing all day long. We're doing *Detective Story* at the Y. I'm playing the shoplifter. It's an exhausting role, believe me." She paused. "We're all Equity players, you understand. This is just between jobs."

"I understand," Carella said.

"How do you like living with a pair of strippers?" Hawes asked.

"Fine," Taffy said. "Gee, what's wrong with strippers? They're swell girls." She paused. "I've been out of work for a long time now. Somebody's got to keep up the rent. They've been swell about it."

"They?" Carella said.

"Barbara and Marla. Of course, Barbara's gone now. You know that. Listen, what does a B-sheet look like?"

"Huh?" Carella said.

"A B-sheet. It's mentioned in the play, it takes place in a detective squadroom, you know."

"Yes, I know."

"Sure, and a B-sheet is mentioned, and our prop man is going nuts trying to figure out what it looks like. Could you send me one?"

"Well, we're not supposed to give out official documents," Hawes said.

"Gee, I didn't know that." She paused. "But we got a real pair of handcuffs. *They're* official, aren't they?"

"Yes. Where'd you get them?"

"Some fellow who used to be a cop. He's got connections." She winked.

"Well, maybe we can send you a B-sheet," Carella said. "If you don't tell anyone where you got it."

"Gee, that would be swell," Taffy answered.

"About your roommate. Barbara. You said she was nice to live with. Didn't she seem a little wild at times?"

"Wild?"

"Yes."

"You mean, did she break dishes? Something like that?"

"No. I meant men."

"Barbara? Wild?"

"Yes. Didn't she entertain a lot of men here?"

"Barbara?" Taffy grinned infectiously. "She never had a man in this apartment all the while I've been living here."

"But she received telephone calls from men, didn't she?"

"Oh, sure."

"And none of these men ever came here?"

"I never saw any. Oh, excuse me. That's the coffee."

She went into the kitchen and returned instantly with the coffeepot and three cardboard containers.

"You'll have to excuse the paper cups," she said, "but we try to keep from washing too many dishes around here. We usually get a mob in every night for coffee, kids from all over who feel like talking or who just feel like sitting on a comfortable chair. We've got a nice place, don't you think?"

"Yes," Carella said.

"I love to make coffee," Taffy said. "I guess I got in

the habit when I was first married. I used to think that was the dream of marriage, do you know? I had the idea that marriage meant you could make a cup of coffee in your own house whenever you wanted to." She grinned again. "I guess that's why I'm divorced right now. Marriage is a lot more than making coffee, I suppose. Still, I like to make coffee."

She poured, went back to the kitchen with the pot, and then returned with cream, sugar, and wooden spoons.

"At these midnight get-togethers," Carella said, "where you make coffee—did Barbara hang around?"

"Oh, sure."

"And she was friendly?"

"Oh, sure."

"But she never brought any men here?"

"Never."

"Never entertained any men here?"

"Never. You see, we only have the three rooms. The kitchen, the living room, and the bedroom. The bedroom has two beds, and this sofa opens into a bed, so that makes three beds. So we had to figure out a sort of a schedule. If one of the girls had a date and she thought she might be asking him in for a drink later, we had to keep the living room free. This really wasn't such a problem because Barbara never brought anyone home. So only Marla and I had to worry about it."

"But Barbara *did* date men?"

"Oh, sure. Lots of them."

"And if she felt like asking someone in for a drink, she didn't ask them in here, is that right?"

"That's right. Some more coffee?"

"No, thank you," Hawes said. He had only taken a sip of the first cup.

"Then where did she take them?" Carella asked.

"I beg your pardon?"

"Her boy friends, Where did she go with them?"

"Oh, all over. Clubs, theaters, wherever they wanted to take her."

"I meant, for that nightcap."

"Maybe she went to their apartments."

"She couldn't have gone to Androvich's apartment," Carella said out loud.

"What was that?"

"There are hotels all over the city, Steve," Hawes said.

"Yeah," Carella said. "Miss Smith, did Barbara ever say anything which would lead you to believe she had *another* apartment?"

"Another one? Why would she need another one? Do you know how much apartments cost in this city?"

"Yes, I do. But did she ever mention anything like that?"

"Not to me, she didn't. Why would she need another apartment?"

"Apparently, Miss Smith, Barbara was seeing a few men and was on . . . rather friendly terms with them. An apartment shared with two other girls might have . . . well, limited her activities somewhat."

"Oh, I see what you mean," Taffy said. She thought about this for a moment. Then she said, "You're talking about Barbara? Bubbles?"

"Yes."

Taffy shrugged. "I never got the idea she was man-crazy. She didn't seem that interested in men."

"She was ready to run off with one when she disappeared," Carella said. "And it's possible she disappeared with a second one."

"Barbara?" Taffy said. "Bubbles?"

"Barbara, yes. Bubbles." Carella paused for a moment. "I wonder if I could use your phone, Miss Smith?"

"Go right ahead. You can use this one, or the extension in the bedroom. Forgive the mess in there. My roommate is a slob."

Carella went into the bedroom.

"Marla told me all about you," Taffy said to Hawes in a whisper.

"She did?"

"Yes. Are you going to call her?"

"Well, I don't know . We've got to wrap up this case first."

"Oh, sure," Taffy agreed. "She's a nice girl. Very sweet."

"Yes, she seemed nice," Hawes said. He felt very uncomfortable all at once.

"Do you work nights?" Taffy asked.

"Sometimes, yes."

"Well, when you're off, why don't you stop by for a cup of coffee?"

"All right, maybe I will."

"Good," Taffy said, and she grinned.

Carella came back into the room. "I just called Androvich's apartment," he said. "Thought he might be able to tell us whether or not Barbara was keeping another place."

"Any luck?"

"He shipped out this morning," Carella said. "For Japan."

Fifteen

THERE IS A CERTAIN LOOK that all big cities take on as five o'clock claims the day. It is a look reserved exclusively for big cities. If you were raised in a small town or a hamlet, you have never seen the look. If you were raised in one of those places that pretend to be huge metropolitan centers but which are in reality only overgrown small towns, you have only seen an imitation of the five-o'clock big city look.

The city is a woman, you understand. It could be nothing but a woman. A small town can be the girl next door or an old man creaking in a rocker or a gangly teen-ager growing out if his dungarees, but the city could be none of these things, the city *is* and can only be a woman. And, like a woman, the city generates love and hate, respect and disesteem, passion and indifference. She is always the same city, always the same woman, but oh the faces she wears, oh the magic guile of this strutting bitch. And if you were born in one of her buildings, and if you know her streets and know her moods, then you love her. Your loving her is not a thing you can control. She has been with you from the start, from the first breath of air you sucked into your lungs, the air mixing cherry blossoms with carbon monoxide, the air of cheap perfume and fresh spring rain, the something in the city air that comes from nothing you can visualize or imagine, the *feel* of city air, the feel of life which you take into your lungs and into your body, this is the city.

And the city is a maze of sidewalks upon which you learned to walk, cracked concrete and sticky asphalt and cobblestones, a hundred thousand corners to turn, a hundred million surprises around each and every one of those corners. This is the city, she grins, she beckons, she cries, her streets are clean sometimes, and sometimes they rustle with fleeing newspapers that rush along the curbstones in time to the beat of her heart. You look at her, and there are so many things to see, so many things to take into your mind and store there, so many things to remember, a myriad things to pile into a memory treasure chest, and you are in love with everything you see, the city can do no wrong, she is your lady love, and she is yours. You remember every subtle mood that crosses her face, you memorize her eyes, now startled, now tender, now weeping; you memorize her mouth in laughter, her windblown hair, the pulse in her throat. This is no casual love affair. She is as much a part of you as your fingerprints.

You are hooked.

You are hooked because she can change her face, this woman, and change her body, and all that was warm and tender can suddenly become cold and heartless— and still you are in love. You will be in love with her forever, no matter how she dresses, no matter how they change her, no matter who claims her, she is the same city you saw with the innocent eyes of youth, and she is yours.

And at five o'clock, she puts on a different look and you love this look, too; you love everything about her, her rages, her sultry petulance, everything; this is total love that seeks no excuses and no reasons. At five o'clock, her empty streets are suddenly alive with life. She has been puttering in a dusty drawing room all day long, this woman, this city, and now it is five o'clock and suddenly she emerges and you are waiting for her, waiting to clutch her in your arms. There is a jauntiness in her step, and yet it veils a weariness, and together they combine to form an image of past and present merged with a future promise. Dusk sits on the skyline, gently touching the saber-edged buildings. Starlight is waiting to bathe her streets in silver. The lights of the city, incandescent and flourescent and neon, are waiting to bracelet her arms and necklace her throat, to hang her with a million gaudy trappings which she does not need. You listen to the hurried purposeful click of her high-heeled pumps and somewhere in the distance there is the growl of a tenor saxophone, far in the distance because this is still five o'clock and the music will not really begin until later, the growl is still deep in the throat. For now, for the moment, there are the cocktail glasses and the muted hum of conversation, the chatter, the light laughter that floats on the air like the sound of shattering glass. And you sit with her, and you watch her eyes, meaningful and deep, and you question her every word, you want to know who she is and what she is, but you will never know. You will love this woman until the day you die, and you will never know her, never come even close to knowing her. Your love is a rare thing bordering on patriotic fervor. For in this city, in this woman, in this big brawling wonderful glittering tender heartless gentle cruel dame of a lady, there is the roar of a nation. If you were born and raised in the city, you cannot think of your country as anything but a giant metropolis. There are no small towns in your nation, there are no waving fields of grain, no mountains, no lakes, no seashores. For you, there is only the city, and she is yours, and love is blind.

Two men in love with the city, Detective Carella and Detective Hawes, joined the throng that rushed along her pavements at five o'clock that afternoon. They did not speak to each other for they were rivals for the same hand, and honorable men do not discuss the woman they both love. They walked into the lobby of the Creo Building and they took the elevator up to the eighteenth floor, and they walked down the deserted corridor to the end of the hall, and then they entered the office of Charles Tudor.

There was no one in the waiting room.

Tudor was locking the door to his inner office as they came in. He turned, still stooping over, the key in the keyhole. He nodded in recognition, finished locking the door, put the keys into his pocket, walked to them with an extended hand and said, "Gentlemen. Any news?"

Carella took the proffered hand. "Afraid not, Mr. Tudor," he answered. "But we'd like to ask you a few more questions."

"Certainly," Tudor said. "You don't mind if we sit here in the waiting room, do you? I've already locked up my private office."

"This'll be fine," Carella said.

They sat on the long couch against the wall covered with strippers.

"You said you were in love with Bubbles Caesar, Mr. Tudor," Carella said. "Did you know that she was seeing at least one other man for certain, and possibly two other men?"

"Barbara?" Tudor asked.

"Yes. Did you know that?"

"No. I didn't."

"Did you see her very often, Mr. Tudor? We're not referring to your business relationship right now."

"Yes. I saw her quite often."

"How often?"

"Well, as often as I could."

"Once a week? Twice a week? More than that? How often, Mr. Tudor?"

"I suppose, on the average, I saw her three or four times a week."

"And what did you do when you saw her, Mr. Tudor?"

"Oh, various things." Tudor gave a small shrug of puzzlement. "What do people do when they go out? Dinner, dancing, the theater, a motion picture, a drive in the country. All those things. Whatever we felt like doing."

"Did you go to bed with her, Mr. Tudor?"

"That is my business," Tudor said flatly. "*And* Barbara's."

"It might be ours, too, Mr. Tudor. Oh, I know, it's a hell of a thing to ask, very personal. We don't like to ask, Mr. Tudor. There are a lot of things we don't like to ask, but unfortunately we have to ask those things, whether we like to or not. I'm sure you can understand."

"No, I'm afraid I cannot," Tudor said with finality.

"Very well, we'll assume you were intimate with her."

"You may assume whatever you wish," Tudor said.

"Where do you live, Mr. Tudor?"

"On Blakely Street."

"Downtown? In The Quarter?"

"Yes."

"Near Barbara's apartment?"

"Fairly close to it, yes."

"Did you ever go to Barbara's apartment?"

"No."

"You never picked her up there?"

"No."

"But you were seeing her?"

"Yes, of course I was seeing her."

"And yet you never went to her apartment. Isn't that a little odd?"

"Is it? I despise the housing facilities of most working girls, Detective Carella. When I call on a young lady, I find the curiosity of her roommates unbearable. And so, whenever a young lady shares an apartment with someone else, I prefer to meet her away from the apartment. That is the arrangement I had with Barbara."

"And apparently an arrangement she preferred. The girls she lived with tell us no man ever came to that apartment to pick her up or take her home. What do you think of that, Mr. Tudor?"

Tudor shrugged. "I am certainly not responsible for Barbara's idiosyncrasies."

"Certainly not. Did Barbara ever come to your apartment?"

"No."

"Why not?"

"I live with my father," Tudor said. "He's a very old man. Practically . . . well, he's very sick. I'm not sure he would have understood Barbara. Or approved of her. And so he never met her."

"You kept her away from your apartment. Is that right?"

"That is correct."

"I see." Carella thought for a moment. He looked at Hawes.

"Where'd you neck, Mr. Tudor?" Hawes asked. "In the back seat of an automobile?"

"That is none of your business," Tudor said.

"Would you know whether or not Barbara had another apartment?" Hawes asked. "Besides the one she shared with the two girls?"

"If she had one, I never saw it," Tudor said.

"You're not married, of course," Carella said.

"No, I'm not married."

"Ever married, Mr. Tudor?"

"Yes."

"What's the status now? Separated? Divorced?"

"Divorced. For a long time now, Detective Carella. At least fifteen years."

"What's your ex-wife's name?"

"Toni Traver. She's an actress. Rather a good one, too."

"She in this city?"

"I'm sure I don't know. I was divorced from her fifteen years ago. I ran into her in Philadelphia once about eight years ago. I haven't seen her since. Nor do I care to."

"You paying her alimony, Mr. Tudor?"

"She didn't want any. She has money of her own."

"Does she know about you and Barbara?"

"I don't know. She couldn't care less, believe me."

"Mmmm," Carella said. "And you didn't know about these two other guys Barbara was seeing, right?"

"Right."

"But surely, if she was seeing them, and if you called for a date or something, she must have said she was busy on that night, no? Didn't you ever ask how come? Didn't you want to know *why* she was busy?"

"I am not a possessive man," Tudor said.

"But you loved her."

"Yes. I loved her, and I still love her."

"Well, how do you feel about it now? Now that you

know she was dating two other man, maybe sleeping
with both of them, how do you feel about it?"

"I . . . naturally, I'm not pleased."

"No, I didn't think you would be. Did you ever meet
a man named Karl Androvich, Mr. Tudor?"

"No."

"How about a man named Mike Chirapadano?"

"No."

"Ever go to The King and Queen?"

"Yes, of course. I sometimes picked Barbara up at
the club."

"Mike was a drummer in the band there."

"Really?"

"Yes." Carella paused. "He seems to have vanished,
Mr. Tudor."

"Really?"

"Yes. At the same time that Barbara did. What do
you think of that?"

"I don't know what to think."

"Think they ran off together?"

"I'm sure I don't know."

"Do you have a black raincoat and umbrella, Mr.
Tudor?"

"No, I don't. A what? A black raincoat, did you
say?"

"Yes, that's what I said."

"No, I don't have one."

"But you do have a raincoat?"

"Yes. A trench coat. It's gray. Or beige. You know, a
neutral sort of . . ."

"And the umbrella? Is it a man's umbrella?"

"I don't have an umbrella. I detest umbrellas."

"Never carry one, right?"

"Never."

"And you don't know of any other apartment Barbara might have kept, right?"

"I don't know of any, no."

"Well, thank you very much, Mr. Tudor," Carella
said. "You've been most helpful."

"Not at all," Tudor answered.

Outside in the hallway, Carella said, "He smells, Cotton. Wait for him downstairs and tail him, will you? I'll be back at the squadroom. I want to check on his exwife, see if I can get a line on her."

"What are you thinking of? Jealousy?"

"Who knows? But some torches have been known to burn for more than fifteen years. Why not hers?"

"The way he put it . . ."

"Sure, but every word he spoke could have been a lie."

"True."

"Tail him. Get back to me. I'll be waiting for your call."

"Where do you expect him to lead me?"

"I don't know, Cotton."

Carella went back to the squadroom. He learned that Toni Traver was a fairly good character actress and that she was at the moment working in a stock playhouse in Sarasota, Florida. Carella talked to her agent who told him that Miss Traver was not accepting alimony from her ex-husband. In fact, the agent said, he and Miss Traver had wedding plans of their own. Carella thanked him and hung up.

At eight P.M. that night, Cotton Hawes called in to report that Tudor had shaken the tail at seven-thirty.

"I'm sorry as hell," he said.

"Yeah," Carella answered.

Sixteen

THE CLOTHES TURNED up the next morning.

They were wrapped in a copy of the *New York Times*. A patrolman in Calm's Point found them in a trash basket. His local precinct called Headquarters because there was a bloodstain on the black raincoat, and Headquarters promptly called the 87th. The clothes were sent to the lab where Grossman inspected them thoroughly.

Besides the raincoat, there was a black flannel suit, a pair of black lisle socks, and a black umbrella.

An examination of the clothing turned up some rather contradictory facts, and all of these were passed on to Carella who studied them and then scratched his head in puzzlement.

To begin with, the bloodstain on the raincoat belonged to the "O" group, which seemed to tie it in with the hands, and to further tie in with Mike Chirapadano whose service record had listed him as belonging to that blood group. But a careful examination of the black suit had turned up a subsequent small bloodstain on the sleeve. And this bloodstain belonged to the "B" group. That was the first contradiction.

The second contradiction seemed puzzling all over again. It had to do with three other stains which were found on the black suit. The first of these was of a hair preparation, found on the inside of the collar where the collar apparently brushed against the nape of the neck. The stain was identified as coming from a tonic called Strike. It was allegedly designed for men who had oily scalps and who did not wish to compound the affliction by using an oily hair tonic.

But side by side with this stain was the second stain, and it had been caused by a preparation known as Dram, which was a hair tonic designed to fight dandruff and dry, flaky scalps. It seemed odd that these two scalp conditions could exist in one and the same man. It seemed contradictory that a person with a dry, flaky scalp would also be a person with an oily scalp. Somehow, the two hair preparations did not seem very compatible.

The third stain on the suit jacket was identified as coming from the selfsame Skinglow cosmetic which had been found in the corner of the airlines bag, and this led to some confusion as to whether a man or a woman had worn the damn suit. Carella concluded that a man had worn it, but that he had embraced a woman wearing Skinglow. This accounted for that stain, but not for the hair tonic stains which were still puzzling and contradictory.

But there were more contradictions. The human hairs that clung to the fiber of the suit, for example. Some were brown and thin. Others were black and thick and short. And still others were black and thin and very long. The very long black ones presumably were left on the suit by the dame who'd worn the Skinglow. That embrace was shaping up as a very passionate one. But the thin brown hairs? And the thick black short ones? Puzzlement upon puzzlement.

About one thing, there was no confusion. There was a label inside the suit jacket, and the label clearly read: *Urban-Suburban Clothes.*

Carella looked up the name in the telephone directory, came up with a winner, clipped on his holster, and left the squadroom.

Cotton Hawes was somewhere in the city glued to Charles Tudor, whose trail he had picked up again early in the morning.

Urban-Suburban Clothes was one of those tiny shops which are sandwiched in between two larger shops and which would be missed entirely were it not for the colorful array of offbeat clothes in the narrow window. Carella opened the door and found himself in a long narrow cubicle which had been designed as a coffin for one man and which now held twelve men, all of whom were pawing through ties and feeling the material of sports coats and holding Italian sports shirts up against their chests. He felt an immediate attack of claustrophobia, which he controlled, and then he began trying to determine which of the twelve men in the shop was the owner. It occurred to him that thirteen was an unlucky number, and he debated leaving. He was carrying the bundle of clothes wrapped in brown paper and the bundle was rather bulky and this did not ease the crowded atmosphere of the shop at all. He squeezed past two men who were passing out cold over the off-orange tint of a sports shirt which had no buttons.

"Excuse me," he said, "excuse me." And he executed an off-tackle run around a group of men who were huddled at the tie rack. The ties, apparently were made of Indian madras in colors the men were declaring to be simultaneously "cool," "wild," and "crazy." Carella felt hot, tamed, and very sane.

He kept looking for the owner of the shop, and finally a voice came at his elbow. "May I help you, sir?" And a body materialized alongside the voice. Carella whirled to face a thin man with a Fu Manchu beard, wearing a tight brown suit over a yellow weskit, and leering like a sex maniac in a nudist camp.

"Yes, yes, you can," Carella said. "Are you the owner of this shop?"

"Jerome Jerralds," the young man said, and he grinned.

"How do you do, Mr. Jerralds?" Carella said. "I'm . . ."

"Trouble?" Jerralds said, eying the bundle of wrapped clothes. "One of our garmets didn't fit you properly?"

"No, it's . . ."

"Did you make the purchase yourself, or was it a gift?"

"No, this . . ."

"You didn't buy the garment yourself?"

"No," Carella said. "I'm a . . ."

"Then it was a gift?"

"No. I'm . . ."

"Then how did you get it, sir?"

"The police lab sent the clothes over," Carella answered.

"The poli—?" Jerralds started, and his hand went up to stroke the Chinese beard, a cat's-eye ring gleaming on his pinky.

"I'm a cop," Carella explained.

"Oh?"

"Yeah. I've got a pile of clothes here. I wonder if you can tell me anything about them."

"Well, I . . ."

"I know you're busy, and I won't take much of your time."

"Well, I . . ."

Carella had already unwrapped the package. There's a label in the suit," he said. "*Urban-Surburban Clothes.* This your suit?"

Jerralds studied it. "Yes, that is our suit."

"How about the raincoat? It looks like the kind of thing you might sell, but the label's been torn out. Is it your coat?"

"What do you mean, it looks like the kind of thing we might sell?"

"Stylish," Carella said.

"Oh, I see."

"With a flair," Carella said.

"Yes, I see."

"Important-looking," Carella said.

"Yes, yes."

"Cool," Carella said. "Wild. Crazy."

"That's our raincoat, all right," Jerralds said.

"How about this umbrella?"

"May I see it, please?"

Carella handed him the tagged umbrella.

"No, that's not ours," Jerralds said. "We try to offer something different in men's umbrellas. For example, we have one with a handle made from a ram's horn, and another fashioned from a Tibetan candlestick which . . ."

"But this one is yours, right?"

"No. Were you interested in . . . ?"

"No, I don't need an umbrella," Carella said. "It's stopped raining, you know."

"Oh, has it?"

"Several days ago."

"Oh. It gets so crowded in here sometimes . . ."

"Yes, I can understand. About this suit and this raincoat, can you tell me who bought them?"

"Well, that would be difficult to . . ." Jerralds stopped. His hand fluttered to the jacket of the suit, landed on the sleeve, scraped at the stain there. "Seem to have got something on the sleeve," he said.

"Blood," Carella answered.

"Wh—?"

"Blood. That's a bloodstain. You sell many of these suits, Mr. Jerralds?"

"Blood, well it's a popular . . . blood? Blood?" He stared at Carella.

"It's a popular number?" Carella said.

"Yes."

"In this size?"

"What size is it?"

"A forty-two."

"That's a big size."

"Yes. The suit was worn by a big man. The raincoat's big, too. Can you remember selling both these items to anyone? There's also a pair of black socks here someplace. Just a second." He dug up the socks. "These look familiar?"

"Those are our socks, yes. Imported from Italy. They have no seam, you see, manufactured all in one . . ."

"Then the suit, the raincoat and the socks are yours. So the guy is either a steady customer, or else someone who stopped in and made all the purchases at one time. Can you think of anyone? Big guy, size forty-two suit?"

"May I see the suit again, please?"

Carella handed him the jacket.

"This is a very popular number," Jerralds said, turning the jacket over in his hands. "I really couldn't estimate how many of them we sell each week. I don't see how I could possibly identify the person who bought it."

"There wouldn't be any serial numbers on it anywhere?" Carella asked. "On the label maybe? Or sewn into the suit someplace?"

"No, nothing like that," Jerralds said. He flipped the suit over and studied both shoulders. "There's a high padding on this right shoulder," he said almost to himself. To Carella, he said, "That's odd because the shoulders are supposed to be unpadded, you see. That's the look we try to achieve. A natural, flowing . . ."

"So what does the padding on that right shoulder mean?"

"I don't know, unless . . .Oh, wait a minute, wait a minute. Yes, yes, I'll bet this is the suit."

"Go ahead," Carella said.

"This gentlemen came in, oh, it must have been shortly after Christmas. A very tall man, very well built. A very handsome man."

"Yes?"

"He . . . well, one leg was slightly shorter than the other. A half-inch, a quarter-inch, something like that. Not serious enough to produce a limp, you understand, but just enough to throw the line of his body slightly out of kilter. I understand there are a great number of men whose . . ."

"Yes, but what about this particular man?"

"Nothing special. Except that we had to build up the right shoulder of the jacket, pad it, you know. To compensate for that shorter leg."

"And this is that jacket?"

"I would think so, yes."

"Who bought it?"

"I don't know."

"He wasn't a regular customer of yours?"

"No. He came in off the street. Yes, I remember now. He bought the suit, and the raincoat, and several pairs of socks, and black knit tie. I remember now."

"But you don't remember his name?"

"No, I'm sorry."

"Do you keep sales slips?"

"Yes, but . . ."

"Do you list a customer's name on the slip?"

"Yes, but . . ."

"But what?"

"This was shortly after Christmas. January. The beginning of January."

"So?"

"Well, I'd have to go through a pile of records to get to . . ."

"I know," Carella said.

"We're very busy now," Jerralds said. "As you can see . . ."

"Yes, I can see."

"This is Saturday, one of our busiest days. I'm afraid I couldn't take the time to . . ."

"Mr. Jerralds, we're investigating a murder," Carella said.

"Oh."

"Do you think you can take the time?"

"Well . . ." Jerralds hesitated. "Very well, would you come into the back of the store, please?"

He pushed aside a curtain. The back of the store was a small cubbyhole piled high with goods in huge cardboard boxes. A man in jockey shorts was pulling on a pair of pants in front of a full-length mirror.

"This doubles as a dressing room," Jerralds explained. "Those trousers are just for you, sir," he said to the half-clad man. "This way; my desk is over here."

He led Carella to a small desk set before a dirty, barred window.

"January, January," he said, "now where would the January stuff be?"

"Is this supposed to be so tight?" the man in trousers said.

"Tight?" Jerralds asked. "It doesn't look at all tight, sir."

"It feels tight to me," the man said. "Maybe I'm not used to these pants without pleats. What do you think?" he asked Carella.

"Looks okay to me," Carella said.

"Maybe I'm just not used to it," the man answered.

"Maybe so."

"They look wonderful," Jerralds said. "That color is a new one. It's sort of off-green. Green and black, a mixture."

"I thought it was gray," the man said, studying the trousers more carefully.

"Well, it looks like gray, and it looks like green, and it also looks like black. That's the beauty of it," Jerralds said.

"Yeah?" The man looked at the trousers again. "It's a nice color," he said dubiously. He thought for a moment, seeking an escape. "But they're too tight," and he began pulling off the trousers. "Excuse me," he said, hopping on one leg and crashing into Carella. "It's a little crowded back here."

"The January file should be . . ." Jerralds touched one temple with his forefinger and knotted his brow. The finger came down like the finger of doom circling in the air and then dived, tapping a carton which rested several feet from the desk. Jerralds opened the carton and began rummaging among the sales slips.

The man threw the trousers onto the desk and said, "I like the color, but they're too tight." He walked to the carton over which he had draped his own trousers and began pulling them on. "I can't stand tight pants, can you?" he asked Carella.

"No," Carella answered.

"I like a lot of room," the man said.

"No, this is February," Jerralds said. "Now where the devil did I put the January slips? Let me think," and again the finger touched his temple, hesitated there until the light of inspiration crossed his bearded face, and then zoomed like a Stuka to a new target. He opened the second carton and pulled out a sheaf of sales slips.

"Here we are," he said. "January. Oh, God, this is going to be awful. We had a clearance sale in January. After Christmas, you know. There are *thousands* of slips here."

"Well, thanks a lot," the man said, secure in his own loose trousers now. "I like a lot of room, you understand."

"I understand," Jerralds said as he leafed through the sales slips.

"I'll drop in again sometime. I'm a cab driver, you see. I need a lot of room. After all, I sit on my ass all day long."

"I understand," Jerralds said. "I think it was the second week in January. After the sale. Let me try those first."

"Well, so long," the cab driver said. "Nice meeting you."

"Take it easy," Carella answered, and the cabbie pushed through the hanging curtains and into the front of the shop.

"Three shirts at four-fifty per . . . no, that's not it. This *is* a job, you know. If you weren't such a nice person, I doubt if I'd . . . one pair of swim trunks at . . . no . . . ties, no . . . one raincoat black one suit charcoal, three pair lisle . . . here it is, here it is," Jerralds said. "I thought so. January tenth. Yes, it was a cash sale."

"And the man's name?"

"It should be on the top of the slip here. It's a little difficult to read. The carbon isn't too clear."

"Can you make it out?" Carella asked.

"I'm not sure. Chirapadano, does that sound like a name? Michael Chirapadano?"

Seventeen

THE LANDLADY SAID, "Are you here again? Where's your redheaded friend?"

"Working on something," Carella said. "I'd like to go through Chirapadano's room again. That okay with you?"

"Why? You got a clue?"

"Maybe."

"He owes me two months' rent," the landlady said. "Come on, I'll take you up."

They walked upstairs. She cleaned the banister with an oily cloth as they went up. She led Carella to the apartment and was taking out the key when she stopped. Carella had heard the sound, too. His gun was already in his hand. He moved the landlady to one side and was backing off against the opposite wall when she whispered, "For God's sake, don't break it in. Use my key, for God's sake!"

He took the key from her, inserted it into the lock, and twisted it as quietly as he could. He turned the knob then and shoved against the door. The door would not budge. He heard a frantic scurrying inside the apartment, and he shouted, "Goddamnit!" and hurled his shoulder against the door, snapping it inward.

A tall man stood in the center of the room, a bass drum in his hands.

"Hold it, Mike!" Carella shouted, and the man threw the bass drum at him, catching him full in the chest, knocking him backward and against the landlady who kept shouting, "I told you not to break it in! Why didn't you use the key!"

The man was on Carella now. He did not say a word.

159

There was a wild gleam in his eyes as he rushed Carella, disregarding the gun in Carella's fist as the landlady screamed her admonitions. He threw a left that caught Carella on the cheek and was drawing back his right when Carella swung the .38 in a side-swiping swing that opened the man's cheek. The man staggered backward, struggling for balance, tripping over the rim of the bass drum and crashing through the skin. He began crying suddenly, a pitiful series of sobs that erupted from his mouth.

"Now you broke it," he said. "Now you went and broke it."

"Are you Mike Chirapadano?" Carella asked.

"That ain't him," the landlady said. "Why'd you break the door in? You cops are all alike! Why didn't you use the key like I told you?"

"I *did* use the damn key," Carella said angrily. "All it did was lock the door. The door was already open. You sure this isn't Chirapadano?"

"Of course I'm sure. How could the door have been open? I locked it myself."

"Our friend here probably used a skeleton key on it. How about that, Mac?" Carella asked.

"Now you broke it," the man said. "Now you went and broke it."

"Broke what?"

"The drum. You broke the damn drum."

"You're the one who broke it," Carella said.

"You hit me," the man said. "I wouldn't have tripped if you hadn't hit me."

"Who are you? What's your name? How'd you get in here?"

"You figure it out, big man."

"Why'd you leave the door unlocked?"

"Who expected anyone to come up here?"

"What do you want here anyway? Who are you?"

"I wanted the drums."

"Why?"

"To hock them."

"Mike's drums?"

"Yes."

"All right, now who are you?"

"What do you care? You broke the bass drum. Now I can't hock it."

"Did Mike ask you to hock his drums?"

"No."

"You were stealing them?"

"I was borrowing them."

"Sure. What's your name?"

"Big man. Has a gun, so he thinks he's a big man." He touched his bleeding face. "You cut my cheek."

"That's right," Carella said. "What's your name?"

"Larry Daniels."

"How do you know Chirapadano?"

"We played in the same band."

"Where?"

"The King and Queen."

"You a good friend of his?"

Daniels shrugged.

"What instrument do you play?"

"Trombone."

"Do you know where Mike is?"

"No."

"But you knew he wasn't here, didn't you? Otherwise you wouldn't have sneaked up here with your skeleton key and tried to steal his drums. Isn't that right?"

"I wasn't stealing them. I was borrowing them. I was going to give him the pawn ticket when I saw him."

"Why'd you want to hock the drums?"

"I need some loot."

"Why don't you hock your trombone?"

"I already hocked the horn."

"You the junkie Randy Simms was talking about?"

"Who?"

"Simms. Randy Simms. The guy who owns The King and Queen. He said the trombone player on the band was a junkie. That you, Daniels?"

"Okay, that's me. It ain't no crime to be an addict. Check the law. It ain't no crime. And I got no stuff on me, so put that in your pipe and smoke it. You ain't got me on a goddamn thing."

"Except attempted burglary," Carella said.

"Burglary, my ass. I was borrowing the drums."

"How'd you know Mike wouldn't be here?"

"I knew, that's all."

"Sure. But how? Do you know where he is right this minute?"

"No, I don't know."

"But you knew he wasn't here."

"I don't know nothing."

"A dope fiend," the landlady said. "I knew it."

"Where is he, Daniels?"

"Why do you want him?"

"We want him."

"Why?"

"Because he owns a suit of clothes that may be connected with a murder. And if you withhold information from us, you can be brought in as an accessory after the fact. Now how about that, Daniels? Where is he?"

"I don't know. That's the truth."

"When did you see him last?"

"Just before he made it with the dame."

"What dame?"

"The stripper."

"Bubbles Caesar?"

"That's her name."

"When was this, Daniels?"

"I don't remember the date exactly. It was around Valentine's Day. A few days before."

"The twelfth?"

"I don't remember."

"Mike didn't show up for work on the night of the twelfth. Was that the day you saw him?"

"Yeah. That's right."

"When did you see him?"

"In the afternoon sometime."

"And what did he want?"

"He told me he wouldn't be on the gig that night, and he give me the key to his pad."

"Why'd he do that?"

"He said he wanted me to take his drums home for him. So when we quit playing that night, that's what I done. I packed up his drums and took them here."

"So that's how you got in today. You still have Mike's key."

"Yeah."

"And that's how you knew he wouldn't be here. He never did get that key back from you, did he?"

"Yeah, that's right." Daniels paused. "I was supposed to call him the next day and we was supposed to meet so I could give him the key. Only I called, and there was no answer. I called all that day, but nobody answered the phone."

"This was the thirteenth of February?"

"Yeah, the next day."

"And he had told you he would be with Bubbles Caesar?"

"Well, not directly. But when he give me the key and the telephone number, he made a little joke, you know? He said, 'Larry, don't be calling me in the middle of the night because Bubbles and me, we are very deep sleepers.' Like that. So I figured he would be making it with Bubbles that night. Listen, I'm beginning to get itchy. I got to get out of here."

"Relax, Daniels. What was the phone number Mike gave you?"

"I don't remember. Listen, I got to get a shot. I mean, now listen, I ain't kidding around here."

"What was the number?"

"For Christ's sake, who remembers? This was last month, for Christ's sake. Look, now look, I ain't kidding here. I mean, I got to get out of here. I know the signs, and this is gonna be bad unless I get . . ."

"Did you write the number down?"

"What?"

"The number. Did you write it down?"

"I don't know, I don't know," Daniels said, but he pulled out his wallet and began going through it, muttering all the while, "I have to get a shot, I have to get fixed, I have to get out of here," his hands trembling as he riffled through the wallet's compartments. "Here," he said at last, "here it is, here's the number. Let me out of here before I puke."

Carella took the card.

"You can puke at the station house," he said.

The telephone number was Economy 8–3165.

At the squadroom, Carella called the telephone company and got an operator who promptly told him she had no record of any such number.

"It may be an unlisted number," Carella said. "Would you please check it?"

"If it's an unlisted number, sir, I would have no record of it."

"Look, this is the police department," Carella said. "I know you're not supposed to divulge . . ."

"It is not a matter of not divulging the number, sir. It is simply that I would have no record of it. What I'm trying to tell you, sir, is that we do *not* have a list labeled 'Unlisted Numbers.' Do you understand me, sir?"

"Yes, I understand you," Carella said. "But the telephone company has a record of it someplace, doesn't it? Somebody pays the damn bill. Somebody *gets* the bill each month. All I want to know is who gets it?"

"I'm sorry, sir, but I wouldn't know who . . ."

"Let me talk to your supervisor," Carella said.

Charles Tudor had begun walking from his home in The Quarter, and Cotton Hawes walked directly behind him. At a respectable distance, to be sure. It was a wonderful day for walking, a day that whetted the appetite for spring. It was a day for idling along and stopping at each and every store window, a day for admiring the young ladies who had taken off their coats and blossomed earlier than the flowers.

Tudor did not idle, and Tudor did not admire. Tudor walked at a rapid clip, his head ducked, his hands thrust into the pockets of his topcoat, a big man who shouldered aside any passerby who got in his way. Hawes, an equally big man, had a tough time keeping up with him. The sidewalks of The Quarter on that lovely Saturday were cluttered with women pushing baby carriages, young girls strutting with high-tilted breasts, young men wearing faded tight jeans and walking with the lope of male dancers, young men sporting beards and paint-smeared sweat shirts, girls wearing leotards over which were Bermuda shorts, old men carrying canvases decorated with pictures of the ocean, Italian housewives from the neighborhood carrying shopping bags bulging with long breads, young actresses wearing make-up to rehearsals in the many little theaters that dotted the side streets, kids playing Johnny-on-the-Pony.

Hawes could have done without the display of humanity. If he were to keep up with Tudor, he'd have to . . .

He stopped suddenly.

Tudor had gone into a candy store on the corner. Hawes quickened his pace. He didn't know whether or not there was a back entrance to the store, but he had lost Tudor the night before, and he didn't want to lose him again. He walked past the candy store and around the corner. There was only one entrance, and he could see Tudor inside making a purchase. He crossed the street quickly, took up a post in the doorway of a tenement, and waited for Tudor to emerge. When Tudor came out, he was tearing the cellophane top from a package of cigarettes. He did not stop to light the cigarette. He lighted it as he walked along, three matches blowing out before he finally got a stream of smoke.

Doggedly, Hawes plodded along behind him.

"Good afternoon, sir, this is your supervisor; may I help you, sir?"

"Yes," Carella said. "This is Detective Carella of the 87th Squad up here in Isola," he said, pulling his rank. "We have a telephone number we're trying to trace, and it seems . . ."

"Did the call originate from a dial telephone, sir?"

"What call?"

"Because if it did, sir, it would be next to impossible to trace it. A dial telephone utilizes automatic equipment and . . ."

"Yes, I know that. We're not trying to trace a call, operator, we're trying to . . ."

"I'm the supervisor, sir."

"Yes, I know. We're . . ."

"On the other hand, if the call was made from a manual instrument, the possibilities of tracing it would be a little better. Unless it got routed eventually through automatic . . ."

"Lady, I'm a cop, and I know about tracing telephone calls, and all I want you to do is look up a number and tell me the party's name and address. That's all I want you to do."

"I see."

"Good. The number is Economy 8–3165. Now would you please look that up and give me the information I want?"

"Just one moment, sir."

Her voice left the line. Carella drummed impatiently on the desk top. Bert Kling, fully recovered, furiously typed up a D.D. report at the adjoining desk.

Tudor was making another stop. Hawes cased the shop from his distant vantage point. It was set between two other shops in a row of tenements, and so the possibility of another entrance was unlikely. If there *was* another entrance, it would not be one accessible to customers of the shop.

Hawes lighted a cigarette and waited for Tudor to make his purchase and come into the street again.

He was in the shop for close to fifteen minutes.

When he came out, he was carrying some white gardenias.

Oh great, Hawes thought, *he's going to see a dame.*

And then he wondered if the dame could be Bubbles Caesar.

"Sir, this is your supervisor."

"Yes?" Carella said. "Have you got . . . ?"

"You understand, sir, that when a person requests an unlisted or unpublished telephone number, we . . ."

"I'm not a person," Carella said, "I'm a cop." He wrinkled his brow and thought that one over for a second.

"Yes, sir, but I'm referring to the person whose telephone number this is. When that person requests an unpublished number, we make certain that he understands what this means. It means that there will be no record of the listing available, and that no one will be able to get the number from anyone in the telephone company, even upon protest of an emergency condition existing. You understand that, sir?"

"Yes, I do. Lady, I'm a cop investigating a murder. Now will you please . . ."

"Oh, I'll give you the information you requested. I certainly will."

"Then what . . . ?"

"But I want you to know that an ordinary citizen could not under any circumstances get the same information. I simply wanted to make the telephone company's policy clear."

"Oh, it's perfectly clear, operator."

"Supervisor," she corrected.

"Yes, sure. Now who's that number listed for, and what's the address?"

"The phone is in a building on Canopy Street. The address is 1611."

"Thank you. And the owner of the phone?"

"No one *owns* our telephones, sir. You realize that our instruments are provided on a rental basis, and that . . ."

"Whose name is that phone listed under, oper—supervisor? Would you please . . .?"

"The listing is for a man named Charles Tudor," the supervisor said.

"Charles Tudor?" Carella said. "Now what the hell . . . ?"

"Sir?" the supervisor asked.

"Thank you," Carella said, and he hung up. He turned to Kling. "Bert," he said, "get your hat."

"I don't wear any," Kling said, so he clipped on his holster instead.

Charles Tudor had gone into 1611 Canopy Street, unlocked the inner vestibule door, and vanished from sight.

Hawes stood in the hallway now and studied the mailboxes. None of them carried a nameplate for Bubbles Caesar or Charles Tudor or Mike Chirapadano or anyone at all with whom Hawes was familiar. Hawes examined the mailboxes again, relying upon one of the most elementary pieces of police knowledge in his second study for the nameplates. For reasons known only to God and psychiatrists, when a person assumes a fictitious name, the assumed name will generally have the same initials as the person's real name. Actually, this isn't a mystery worthy of supernatural or psychiatric secrecy. The simple fact is that a great many people own monogrammed handkerchiefs, or shirts, or suitcases, or dispatch cases, or whatever. And if a man named Benjamin Franklin who has the initials B. F. on his bags and his shirts and his underwear and maybe tattooed on his forehead should suddenly register in a hotel as George Washington, a curious clerk might wonder whether or not Benjy came by his B. F. luggage in an illegal manner. Since a man using an assumed name is a man who is not anxious to attract attention, he will do everything possible to make things easier for himself. And so he will use the initials of his real name in choosing an alias.

One of the mailboxes carried a nameplate for a person called Christopher Talley.

It sounded phony, and it utilized the C. T. initials, and so Hawes made a mental note of the apartment number: 6B.

Then he pressed the bell for apartment 2A, waited for the answering buzz that released the inner door lock, and rapidly climbed the steps to the sixth floor. Outside apartment 6B, he put his ear to the door and listened. Inside the apartment, a man was talking.

"Barbara," the man said, "I brought you some more flowers."

In the police sedan, Carella said, "I don't get it, Bert. I just don't get it."

"What's the trouble?" Kling asked.

"No trouble. Only confusion. We find a pair of hands, and the blood group is identified as 'O', right?"

"Right."

"Okay. Mike Chirapadano is in that blood group. He's also a big guy, and he vanished last month, and so that would make him a good prospect for the *victim,* am I right?"

"Right," Kling said.

"Okay. But when we find the clothes the murderer was wearing, it turns out they belonged to Mike Chirapadano. So it turns out that he's a good prospect for the *murderer,* too."

"Yeah?" Kling said.

"Yeah. Then we get a line on Bubbles Caesar's hideout, the place she and Chirapadano used, the place we're going to right now . . ."

"Yeah?"

"Yeah; and it turns out the phone is listed for Charles Tudor, Bubbles' agent. Now how does that figure?"

"There's 1611 up ahead," Kling said.

Standing in the hallway, Hawes could hear only the man's voice, and the voice definitely belonged to Charles Tudor. He wondered whether or not he should crash the apartment. Scarcely daring to breathe, trying desperately to hear the girl's replies, he kept his ear glued to the wood of the door, listening.

"Do you like the flowers, Barbara?" Tudor said.

There was a pause. Hawes listened, but could hear no reply.

"I didn't know whether or not you liked gardenias, but we have so many of the others in here. Well, a beautiful woman should have lots of flowers."

Another pause.

"You *do* like gardenias?" Tudor said. "Good. You look beautiful today, Barbara. Beautiful. I don't think I've ever seen you looking so beautiful. Did I tell you about the police?"

Hawes listened for the reply. He thought instantly of Marla Phillips' tiny voice, and he wondered if all big girls were naturally endowed with the same voices. He could not hear a word.

"You don't want to hear about the police?" Tudor said. "Well, they came to see me again yesterday. Asking about you and me. And Mike. And asking whether or not I owned a black raincoat and umbrella. I told them I didn't. That's the truth, Barbara. I really don't own a black raincoat, and I've never liked umbrellas. You didn't know that, did you? Well, there a lot of things you don't know about me. I'm a very complex person. But we have lots of time. You can learn all about me. You look so lovely. Do you mind my telling you how beautiful you look?"

This time, Hawes heard something.

But the sound had come from behind him, in the hallway.

He whirled, drawing his .38 instantly.

"Put up the gun, Cotton," Carella whispered.

"Man, you scared the hell out of me!" Hawes whispered back. He peered past Carella, saw Kling standing there behind him.

"Tudor in there?" Carella asked.

"Yeah. He's with the girl."

"Bubbles?"

"That's right."

"Okay, let's break it open," Carella said.

Kling took up a position to the right of the door, Hawes to the left. Carella braced himself and kicked in the lock. The door swung open. They burst into the room with their guns in their hands, and they saw Charles Tudor on his knees at one end of the room.

And then they saw what was behind Tudor, and each of the men separately felt identical waves of shock and terror and pity, and Carella knew at once that they would not need their guns.

Eighteen

THE ROOM WAS FILLED with flowers. Bouquets of red
roses and white roses and yellow roses, smaller bouquets
of violets, long-stemmed gladioli, carnations, gardenias,
rhododendron leaves in water-filled vases. The room
was filled with the aroma of flowers—fresh flowers and
dying flowers, flowers that were new, and flowers that
had lost their bloom. The room was filled with the overwhelming scent of flowers and the overwhelming stench
of something else.

The girl, Bubbles Caesar, lay quite still on the table
around which the flowers were massed. Her black hair
trailed behind her head, her long body was clad only in
a nightgown, her slender hands were crossed over her
bosom. A ruby necklace circled her throat. She lay on
the table and stared at the ceiling, and she saw nothing,
because she was stone cold dead and she'd been that
way for a month and her decomposing body stank to
high heaven.

Tudor, or his knees, turned to look at the detectives.

"So you found us," he said quietly.

"Get up, Tudor."

"You found us," he repeated. He looked at the dead
girl again. "She's beautiful, isn't she?" he asked of no
one. "I've never known anyone as beautiful as she."

In the closet, they found the body of a man. He was
wearing only his undershorts. Both of his hands had
been amputated.

The man was Mike Chirapadano.

Oh, he knew that she was dead; he knew that he had
killed them both. They stood around him in the squad-

room, and they asked their questions in hushed voices because it was all over now and, killer or not, Charles Tudor was a human being, a man who had loved. Not a cheap thief, and not a punk, only a murderer who had loved. But yes, he knew she was dead. Yes, he knew that. Yes, he knew he had killed her, killed them both. He knew.

And yet, as he talked, as he answered the almost whispered questions of the detectives, it seemed he did not know, it seemed he wandered from the cruel reality of murder to another world, a world where Barbara Caesar was still alive and laughing. He crossed the boundary line into this other world with facility, and then recrossed it to reality, and then lost it again until there were no boundaries any more, there was only a man wandering between two alien lands, a native of neither, a stranger to both.

"When they called me from the club," he said, "when Randy Simms called me from the club, I didn't know what to think. Barbara was usually very reliable. So I called her apartment, the one she shared with the other girls, and I spoke to one of her roommates, and the roommate told me she hadn't seen her since early that morning. This was the twelfth, February twelfth; I'll remember that day as long as I live, it was the day I killed Barbara."

"What did you do after you spoke to the roommate, Mr. Tudor?"

"I figured perhaps she'd gone to the other apartment, the one on Canopy Street."

"Were you paying for that apartment, Mr. Tudor?"

"Yes. Yes, I was. Yes. But it was *our* apartment, you know. We shared it. We share a lot of things, Barbara and I. We like to do a lot of things together. I have tickets for a show next week. A musical. She likes music. We'll see that together. We do a lot of things together."

The detectives stood in a silent knot around him. Carella cleared his throat.

"Did you go to the apartment, Mr. Tudor? The one on Canopy Street?"

"Yes, I did. I got there sometime around ten o'clock. In the night. It was nighttime. And I went right upstairs, and I used my key, and I . . . well, she was there. With this man. This man was touching her. In our apartment. Barbara was in *our* apartment with another man." Tudor shook his head. "She shouldn't do things like that. She knows I love her. I bought her a ruby necklace for Valentine's Day. Did you see the necklace? It's quite beautiful. She wears it very well."

"What did you do when you found them, Mr. Tudor?"

"I . . . I was shocked. I . . . I . . . I wanted to know. She . . . she told me I didn't own her. She told me she was free, she said nobody owned her, not me, not . . . not the man she was with and . . . and . . . and not Karl either, she said, not Karl, I didn't even know who Karl was. She . . . she said she had promised this Karl she'd go away with him, but he didn't own her either, nobody owned her, she said, and . . . and . . ."

"Yes, Mr. Tudor?"

"I couldn't believe it because . . . well, I love her. You know that. And she was saying these terrible things, and this man, this Mike, stood there grinning. In his underwear, he was in his underwear, and she had on a nightgown I'd given her, the one *I'd* given her. I . . . I . . . I hit him. I kept hitting him, and Barbara laughed, she laughed all the while I was hitting him. I'm a very strong man, I hit him and I kept banging his head against the floor and then Barbara stopped laughing and she said, 'You've killed him.' I . . . I . . ."

"Yes?"

"I took her in my arms, and I kissed her and . . . and . . . I . . . my hands . . . her throat . . . she didn't scream . . . nothing . . . I simply squeezed and . . . and she . . . she . . . she went limp in my arms. It was his fault I thought, his fault, touching her, he shouldn't have touched her, he had no right to touch the woman I loved and so I . . . I went into the kitchen looking for a . . . a knife or something. I found a meat cleaver in one of the drawers and I . . . I went into the other room and cut off both his hands." Tudor paused.

"For touching her. I cut off his hands so that he would never touch her again." His brow wrinkled with the memory. "There . . . there was a lot of blood. I . . . picked up the hands and put them in . . . in Barbara's overnight bag. Then I dragged his body into the closet and tried to clean up a little. There . . . there was a lot of blood all over."

They got the rest of the story from him in bits and pieces. And the story threaded the boundary line, wove between reality and fantasy. And the men in the squadroom listened in something close to embarrassment, and some of them found other things to do, downstairs, away from the big man who sat in the hard-backed chair and told them of the woman he'd loved, the woman he still loved.

He told them he had begun disposing of Chirapadano's body last week. He had started with the hands, and he decided it was best to dispose of them separately. The overnight bag would be safe, he'd thought, because so many people owned similar bags. He had decided to use that for the first hand. But it occurred to him that identification of the body could be made through the finger tips, and so he had sliced those away with a kitchen knife.

"I cut myself," he said. "When I was working on the fingertips. Just a small cut, but it bled a lot. My finger."

"What type blood do you have, Mr. Tudor?" Carella asked.

"What? B, I think. Yes, B. Why?"

"That might explain the contradictory stain on the suit, Steve," Kling said.

"What?" Tudor said. "The suit? Oh, yes. I don't know why I did that, really. I don't know why. It was just something I had to do, something I . . . I just *had* to do."

"What was it you had to do, Mr. Tudor?"

"Put on his clothes," Tudor said. "The dead man's. I . . . I put on his suit, and his socks, and I wore his raincoat, and I carried his umbrella. When I went out to . . . to get rid of the hands." He shrugged. "I don't know why. Really, I don't know why." He paused. "I threw the clothes away as soon as I realized you knew about them. I went all the way out to Calm's Point, and I threw them in a trash basket." Tudor looked at the circle of faces around him. "Will you be keeping me much longer?" he asked suddenly.

"Why, Mr. Tudor?"

"Because I want to get back to Barbara," he told the cops.

They took him downstairs to the detention cells, and then they sat in the curiously silent squadroom.

"There's the answer to the conflicting stuff we found on the suit," Kling said.

"Yeah."

"They both wore it. The killer *and* the victim."

"Yeah."

"Why do you suppose he put on the dead man's clothes?" Kling shuddered. "Jesus, this whole damn case . . ."

"Maybe he knew," Carella said.

"Knew what?"

"That he was a victim, too."

Miscolo came in from the Clerical Office. The men in the squadroom were silent.

"Anybody want some coffee?" he asked.

Nobody wanted any coffee.